Enjoy the Rush!

Sugar Rush: Love's Liberation

Yolanda Blake

June 2006

Cover Design by
Jackie Ray Armstrong, Jr.

Printed in the United States of America

For booking or other information please call (301) 523-0227.

Sugar Rush: Love's Liberation is a work of fiction. Names and some
incidents are either the products of the author's imagination or used
fictitiously, and any resemblance to actual persons, living or dead, events,
or locales are entirely coincidental. Some events were inspired by life
experiences.

ISBN: 1-4196-0364-7

To order additional copies, please contact us.
BookSurge, LLC
www.booksurge.com
1-866-308-6235
orders@booksurge.com

YOLONDA D. COLEMAN

SUGAR RUSH: LOVE'S LIBERATION

2005

Sugar Rush: Love's Liberation

I sleep but my heart is awake. It is the voice of my beloved! He knocks, saying, "Open for me, my sister, my love, my dove, my perfect one…"

-Song of Songs 5:2

Sugar Rush: Love's Liberation is dedicated to my Mommy, Michelle D. Bradford. God used you to create me. Thanks for believing in me when others were puzzled by my vision. Your encouragement helped me to go forward. God's light shined through you. Thanks for always loving me. I love you. I miss you. Chop! Chop!

SWIMMING WITH THE DOLPHINS
For My Mommy

The heart's water will run forever
In the form of a crescent moon
She smiles knowing we're okay
The sun shines at high noon.

In her father's kingdom
She has her dream home
With thoughts of nothing bothersome
And river beds of gold.

An angel has her wings
But they flap in the sea
She's swimming with the dolphins
Waving at us effortlessly.

She told us not to worry.
She begged us not to cry.
She knew her time in glory
Was well beyond the sky.

Her heart was always pure and
As purple as royalty
God sacrificed his son, Jesus
And He let her suffering cease.

Her spirit continues on
Through you, me, and others
When you look into the ocean blue
Know that she will always be covered.

Jesus paid the price for her
His name was the last sound we heard.
God was the one who shared her with us
She lived by His word.

Rest in peace, mommy. We're still cheering your name.

PART I
THE SUGAR

CHAPTER ONE
New Buds

Untouched by the sunlight or the rays of the moon,
Clouds hovered at noon and the smell of roses faded.
A stale flower sat on my coffee table.

I was a fool for love wandering in the deep green of the
trees
Hearing the whispers of the truth
But denial set and devoured me
I thought it was only me in the woods.
Through prayer, I confronted the depths of the jungle

And maybe, just maybe, I will run into a rose garden
That won't die.
I will plant seeds that will grow.
Beautiful arrangements will sing.
Leaves will dance.
And I will smile at the new buds emerging through my soil.

It was a Friday going into a Saturday when my world began to flip inside out. The girls and I were celebrating the end of another week. My hair was tight. There wasn't a strand standing lonely on my head that night. I was looking fine in my baby blue, two-piece outfit wrapped around my brown sugar frame. There were slits on each side of my pants to keep me cool from the moisture in Blackplatinum Café. No natural disaster could take my breath away. Having already blown the elements of the universe into my being, I was earth, wind, and fire with a splash of water to maintain the tranquility of my surroundings.

I was babysitting my cranberry juice at our favorite table. Cita and Erica had their usual apple martinis while waiting for the band to get fired up for their next set. Cita made jokes about my juvenile mixture. I smiled knowing that it was not the drink that made a man take a second stare. It was my lips affixed to the rim of the glass that lured him into my web. He'd become curious about the words I might release into the atmosphere. My thought process may have somehow given him a reason to fall in love with me. However, I found comfort in my single world and was trying to avoid love's contact or so I thought. The only thing a man could do for me was wine me, dine me, romance me, and leave me alone.

"You know what you are Dawlee?" Erica asked with a southern drawl. "You're a spida woman."

"A spider woman? How so?"

"Gurl, when you like somebody you spin this alluring web of seduction. Then he fawls for you. Once you have a slight suspicion 'bout his intentions, whoosh, he's pushed out of yo territory."

"Can you really blame me after what I've been through?"

"Dolly that thang with JP was years ago," Cita said swiftly with a Creole tongue.

"Well it still hurts and I have to be cautious. I don't want any more dark episodes in my life. I stop them before a guy makes a fool of himself and me," I mustered to say through pouting lips.

Dating, for me, was like playing the lotto. The odds of me having a quality date in the Washington, D.C. area were slim. I've had my heart broken more times than I care to count. My tolerance level trailed at a negative zero. I was tired of figuring out who was true and who wore masks behind love's veil. Cita and Erica think I use my work to fill the void meant for a man and as a joke bought me a vibrator.

"You need a lil wiggle in your life, honey," Cita said to me while moving in a snake like motion.

As soon as they left me alone with it, I looked at that thing for ten minutes trying to figure out what to do with it, tossed it in the garbage, and booted my computer to see what was hot on the market. I was too busy trying to make money to worry about sex. Although it would be nice to have someone or something to hold on to in the middle of the night, bills still had to be paid.

I do enjoy the company of a man. I just didn't make the men I see a part of my daily routine for any particular length of time. Real estate became my man. I couldn't afford to spend any more of my years being a victim of love. I seemingly had a sign attached to my forehead that welcomed the unemployed, convicted felons, six baby-mama drama having, *I am cave man feed me now* men into my life. It was rare that I would meet a companion with sincere intentions.

As a result of being a loser magnet, I decided to live vicariously through Cita's relationships and Erica's upcoming wedding to experience the mush of love. I was trying to minimize the risks of getting hurt by watching my girls pick up where I left off some years back. I had enough of the humdrum.

Just as Erica was about to analyze me in more detail, a sudden breeze blew in my direction. The smell of fresh bait captured my attention. On the stage of Blackplatinum Café stood a midnight dream at 11:45pm. The sound of chimes echoed throughout the jazz club. The usual band members were getting in place just as the cutie patootey in all black graced the microphone with his heavy, baritone voice.

"How's everyone tonight?" he asked while strapping on his instrument.

My mouth was agape. Every drop of my berry mixture evaporated into my soul. I was bone dry. He left me thirsty wanting to know who he was and how he walked into my comfort zone. Nonetheless, I kept my composure because just a few seconds shy of five minutes ago I was talking smack. I had to be cool in front of my girls. The challenge to do so appeared all over my face. His presence had me open.

The shadow man began to step into the spotlight. He appeared to be six feet tall with a perfectly tapered hairline. His mustache connected to his neatly trimmed goatee that extended from the corners of his lips to his chin. His eyes were a cocoa brown. He was hot chocolate personified and I became warm inside just looking at him.

"Ladies and gentlemen," Midnight began while looking

around the room. "welcome to Blackplatinum's members-only hours."

It seemed as if he was staring directly at me and extending a private invitation for me to listen to him play melodies in my ear.

"Until four, The Platinum Band will play your favorites from Coltrane to Kenny G and I have the distinct honor of making love to your ears with my saxophone."

He was the new lead saxophonist the club had been buzzing about for the past three weeks. I was usually gone by the time the late night set began. On this night, I decided to stay because my last settlement appointment ran a little longer than expected. I wanted to get in as much chill time with my girls before I hit the pavement again. Seeing the subject of the gossip made my stay worthwhile. My innocent attempts to just relax, enjoy the music, and come up with new marketing strategies to target larger clients were put aside because Midnight had given me a new reason to pay attention to the stage. Watching him became a selfish act. I sat up with ears perked and ready to receive his next words. He had my total attention.

"Since we're all here on a first name basis, you can call me Blacksax." He started blowing sporadic tunes into his woodwind instrument. The crowd roared with appreciation. Temperature rising and body melting, I finally closed my mouth and inhaled. Erica pinched my shoulder and I instantly came out of his musical wonderland.

"Hey, Spida Woman? Stay focused," Erica chuckled while playing with her butterfly hair clip. "You know these women are gonna be throwin' Lady Sunshine his way and you ain't gonna give him any." Hmm, maybe she was right. However, Midnight and Lady Sunshine could always come together without the parting of her rays. His rocket didn't have to enter earth's atmosphere to explore terrain. For the moment, I enjoyed looking at him and dreaming of the possibilities. It was as close to the fantasy as I would get, at least until the band finished playing.

CHAPTER TWO
Saxophone Melodies

I can play with a cordless phone attached to my heart.
Sound waves travel swiftly through the air to send you
messages and
Tell stories of melted brown sugar and butter.
I ask, "What's cookin', baby?"
Creating scores of untold secrets while waiting to discover
you,
I uncover your dreams, my sleeping Goddess.
I fill your head like sand in an hourglass.
Time shifts with each melody I play for you
While hoping to hold on to the memory.
I blow.
You hear me.
We flow.
If only you'll pick up and receive me
As I play the score to your heart.
Please, open the door.

The house lights were up and the crowd was in place. I was in the nation's capital ready to blow the roof off Blackplatinum Café. By day I'm Gerald Washington, magazine publisher. By night, I am Blacksax, the marauder of melodies. I play the saxophone and woo anyone who walks into Georgia Avenue's finest jazz club.

I relocated from Florida and started a quarterly literary magazine in a one-bedroom condo in D.C.. *Block Writers* is now in a separate facility on U Street thanks to my dedicated staff and a few grants. I wanted to be in the midst of the next generation of Harlem Renaissance writers. I know. I know. Harlem is in New York City. I just couldn't pay a Big Apple mortgage with my Little Johnny Apple Seeds. D.C. was as close as I was going to get to the Mecca of writers. Besides, there was plenty of raw talent in the city in order for me to gain capital. I was blessed to have my homeboy from college to set up the computer networking system for my office pro bono. Moses was an IT Master. He was one of many resources to help me with the start up of *Block Writers.*

The magazine's subscribers came mostly from metropolitan areas on the east coast. Many high school and college creative writing classes were our primary readers. There was, however, always room for improvement.

I'm a hands-off CEO. I remain low key and let the writers stand in the limelight. My staff is encouraged to explore and embrace their creativity. I trust they will keep *Block Writers* positive by producing quality work that will keep the checks rolling and me out of the courtroom. Monday through Friday they rotate the wheels of the publishing machine. I keep

Block Writers financially afloat. Occasionally, I'll contribute a few poems or some commentary in one of the sections. Friday nights, however, are my moments in the spotlight as a musician; and there was one night in particular that began to change my life.

It was my third set at Blackplatinum Café's members-only night and I was hyped. They say three is a charm. When the curtains opened, I saw the reason my soul danced with anticipation. She sat in the third row bordered by two other ladies. Her hair was long and flowing passed her shoulders. Her eyes twinkled even from the dimly lit candles on the table. I pretended not to notice her, but found it challenging to do so while checking out that one leg laying seductively over the other in her Carolina blue pants. There was a slit on the side. I had a sneak peek of her right thigh from the center stage. She was tapping her feet to the sound of the music and the slit constantly winked at me. I enjoyed watching her move every limb of her body. She was figurative language in motion.

Like the sound of ocean waves splashing against rocks, her presence mesmerized me. Her beauty was a ray of sunshine dancing to my rhythm. Her soul called to me and mine played a silent tune for her to hear. While on stage, I played the sax with my eyes closed. I was envisioning our first encounter. I imagined the lovely melody we'd make without sounding a word.

The band and I played for what seemed an endless two hours before taking a break. I wiped my brow and made a bee-line to the bar.

"Hey, Jimmy. How ya doin' tonight?"

"I guess I'll make it I reckon. The usual, Black?"

"Club soda, man. And uh Jimmy," I began while scoping

out my chocolate Jessica Rabbit, "let me get another one of whatever that lady is having."

"You talkin' 'bout Dolly?"

"Is Dolly the honey wearing the hell outta that blue near the stage?"

"That's Doll."

"Then you got it! I'm fixin' to make my move."

I paid Jimmy and took the drinks. I had a small window to impress this lady and leave with a number before the end of the night. Time slowed down with each step I made toward Dolly's table. I smiled at club goers who complimented me on the show. The smile grew wider upon reaching my destination. One of her girlfriends tapped her to let her know that I was coming her way. Seeing them together reminded me of me and my boys back home in Auburndale. In slow motion, she flipped her hair away from her face and positioned herself to turn around.

"Bonsoir," one of her friends greeted me while pushing her thick hair behind her ears. The other was scanning me with her eyes. As tough as she tried to look, the butterfly clip that held her short hair in place gave away her innocence. Her nonverbal communication just let me know she had her girl's back if I said something stupid.

"Dolly, I have less than a minute to give you this," I began while handing her a glass of cranberry juice, "and to convince you to stay until the end of the show so we can talk."

She smiled a priceless smile and said, "Thank you for the drink." She turned back to face her friends.

I kept my cool but didn't stay and wait like a puppy after a bone. I let out a brief laugh and headed back to the stage. When I heard my name being called, I slowed the pace of my walk and then stopped without turning around.

"Oh and Sax," Dolly began, "if you can come up with something original before the clock strikes four, consider the offer sealed."

I nodded because I was confident I could hold up my end of the deal. I just hoped she didn't renege on hers.

For the next hour, I played as if my life depended on it. I didn't look in her direction while my hands caressed my instrument. I wanted her to understand the messages I was sending through my music. I wanted her to know that I was gently explosive with my hands. The saxophone screamed in ecstasy. Every note played was perfect and complimented the other instruments in the background. The thump from the drums was the heartbeat of the song. It was my motivation. I know she heard the score because my soul felt hers. By 3:50am, I was ready to have her blanketed in my musical review.

I turned just enough to face the band and the audience at the same time and asked, "Hey fellaz, do you mind if I take the last ten minutes to share a little sumpthin' sumpthin' with these lovely people tonight?" Jupiter, the drummer, gave me the go-ahead to proceed. He got his nickname because his skills are out of this world. I took a sip from my glass and prepared to collect my winnings. Dolly sat patiently and for the first time since speaking with her I looked directly in her eyes. I was locked on my target as I spoke to the audience.

"Blackplatinum Café, you've been a wonderful audience tonight. So, let me send you off with a new tune I call *Doll's House.*"

The corners of her lips stretched into a smile. Dolly was impressed. To maintain my position, I never took my eyes off her. She needed to feel more important than anyone else in that room. It was my duty to pretend that the space in Blackplatinum Café was occupied only by Dolly, my saxophone, and me.

I played flawlessly while the band accompanied me. The audience gave us a standing ovation. At the end of the show, the band and I greeted those who rushed to the stage to chat with us. There was a line of women waiting for me. Although I was only interested in the attention of one lady, I spent a few minutes shaking hands, hugging those who extended arms toward me, and took a few business cards only to quickly stash them in my back pocket. Of all the dimes vying for my attention that night, none compared to my caramel dream. I tried earnestly to attend to my fans and cleared a path to get to Dolly at the same time. My efforts were in vain. She was gone. At first I was disappointed. Then again, I felt challenged.

"Yo, Black!" Jimmy called from the bar. "Honey in blue left you a note."

I took the slip of purple paper from Jimmy's hand. He continued to wipe the counter. I read the note written in blue ink. The sweet fragrance that once graced the lining of my nose was all over it. My heart was happy.

Sax,

Thanks for erecting my house. We'll speak soon.

-Dolly

CHAPTER THREE
Cat Chasing

I strayed away far enough to be seen.
I casually dismissed your request to speak with me.
When the horn plays, the cat sways.
The pursuit of happiness is in the chase.
Are you ready to sweat?
Are you able to find me among cat pack?
Or will I give you enough yarn to hang yourself?

I'm such a tease. I should have stayed to chat with Sax. The thrill of the chase is exciting. I felt that if he really wanted to get in touch with me, he'd find another way to convince me to give up my phone number.

"You're no good, Darlene Hunter. Half the women in Blackplatinum would have killed for Sax to dedicate a song to them and here you are playin' games. How old will you be next week?" Cita shook her head with closed fists on her imagination.

"Twenty-nine, thank you," I retorted while doing the colored girl neck roll.

"Actin' like a twelve year old."

"Forget you!" I hit Erica on the shoulder.

"Obviously you've been doing a lot of forgetting tonight," a male voice interjected. Sax stood behind me with his arms folded across his chest. I wondered how much of our conversation he heard. Clearly I was caught, but I had to play off my guilt.

"Whatever do you mean?" I covered my mouth with fingers spread out in a fan. Smoothing out his mustache between his thumb and index finger Sax said, "Well, you're breaching a contract."

"Oh yeah? How so?" I bit my bottom lip while waiting for his response.

"We had a verbal agreement and you failed to hold up your end of the deal. I played my soul for you and I was left with remnants of your lovely fragrance lingering on a slip of purple paper." He waved my note in the air. I smiled and raised my eyebrow. "I can either have you sued or you can meet me for lunch tomorrow, Miss Lady."

Cita and Erica snickered. I was apprehensive about taking the bait until I looked into Gerald's eyes. They told a story of triumph, power, and passion. It was as though he beckoned for me to take a stroll through his soul. The energy between us was something else but I had to maintain my composure. I stayed the course.

"I don't even know your true identity. How about an introduction?"

"My name is Gerald. Gerald A. Washington is my real name," he said with confidence while extending his hand to shake mine.

"Darlene Hunter."

The girls were getting restless. "Okay Doll, we're outta here, gal," Cita remarked.

"Oh, I'm sorry guys. Gerald, this is Cita and Erica."

They gave me the *whatever* stare but smiled at Gerald and shook his hand.

"I'll see you two tomorrow?"

"Mmmm hmmm. Don't be late. We have an appointment at the boutique at four," Erica said with a smirk.

"Do you ladies need me to walk you to your cars?" Gerald started towards them.

"I think we'll be okay. Thanks anyway," Cita replied.

"Well, goodnight, ladies."

"Byyyyyyyye," Cita and Erica sang in unison while waving and walking away.

There was an awkward stillness between us. The Georgia Avenue traffic was our background music as our eyes met again on some unexplainable cosmic wave. What seemed to be an eternity was actually more like a quickie first thing in the morning, brief but satisfying. Gerald made the first move to break our silence.

"So where's your car?" Gerald asked while blowing warm air into his fists.

"The Silver Bullet is right there," I answered and pointed to my Mustang parked near the corners of Georgia and Florida Avenues. We slowly walked in the direction of my ride.

"Thanks for my song. It was nice," sincere gratitude came from my lips. It really was a beautiful song. The sexiest instrument was played by the sexiest man in Blackplatinum that night, and I was the recipient of his love notes.

"If it was so nice, why'd you leave?"

"I don't know. I was ready to go home?" I shrugged my shoulders as if to seem uncertain. A smirk appeared on my face. I knew he didn't buy my excuse.

"You didn't seem ready to go home a few minutes ago."

"Oh...well...I guess I was just catching my second wind."

"Okay. I'll let you slide with that one. For now. But you have to make it up to me. Lunch. Tomorrow."

"I have to work."

"What kinda work do you do on a Saturday, lady?"

"I'm sorry Gerald, I don't know you well enough to share my personal affairs."

"Well let me ask you this..."

"I'm listening."

"Do ordinary people see you enter your place of employment?"

"Yes."

"If I was a tourist taking pictures in your general direction and you showed up in my shots would you sue me?"

"No."

"Then sweetheart, what you do is not personal. It's business and that makes it a public affair, not private."

"Clever, but I'm still not telling you my line of business."

We finally reached my vehicle and he leaned against the passenger's side with folded arms.

"Can you handle all this?" he asked.

I was sure he wasn't talking about the car. I fed into his innuendo since he needed the satisfaction.

"I can hold my own, Mr. Washington. Don't let my femininity fool you. Besides, it only has the power of a horse. I can handle the ride," I said slyly and winked at him.

With a grin, he said, "In that case, let me open the door to your chariot, my lady." I used my electronic key to unlock the doors, and Gerald rushed to the driver's side to help me in.

A few ladies who had just exited the café crossed the street. They looked our way. Gerald got the smiles and I got the cutting eyes and whispers. I expected nothing less. I couldn't help it if I caught his attention. Well, sure I could. If I had come into Blackplatinum with bumper rollers and slippers on all the girls would greet me with laughs. I dress to impress when I cross the threshold of the palace I call home. I never wanted to miss an opportunity to look good for business or pleasure.

My midnight dream was coming to an end. I wanted to give him my phone number but thought it would be wise to wait. After suffering from a series of tumultuous relationships, I usually give guys a couple of chances to pursue me for a first date. Mr. Washington needed an adventure. I wanted an orchestrated chase.

The Silver Bullet hummed and I drove off. Dawn was soon to come and I was anxious to see how big the sun would smile if Gerald and I pranced under its rays. Our song didn't play on this night. I was confident we would have another chance to meet.

Yet, I was patient enough to wait until I put on the right dancing shoes. I only prayed that Gerald was able to keep up with the beat.

CHAPTER FOUR
Gone Fishing

Like a flash from the sky,
She illuminated my soul.
She kept me jolted while time stood still.
My quest was in vain, but only for a moment.
My angelfish may swim
But only to my shore.
I will let the cool water splash
On her scales until they soften and become soft.
She will be flesh of my flesh.

I was certain that beneath her hard shell Dolly housed a warm heart. I can't blame her for being cautious. She didn't know me from a hole in the wall. At the same time, I never had a problem getting a date on the second attempt. I realized I was dealing with a different type of woman, but I kept my bait on the hook. She wasn't going to get too far before this fisherman reeled her in for the taking.

I returned from the front of Blackplatinum to pack up my instrument and bid my fellow band members adieu. Jupiter and I were heading out together. It was almost five o'clock in the morning and this cat was wearing dark shades as if he was the new recruit in the *Matrix*.

"Neo, you are the one," I said jokingly in my best attempt to sound like Laurence Fishburne.

"Man, I know you're not talking with yo black leather on in September lookin' like you're a part of the *Trench Coat Mafia*," Jupiter teased while slapping me on the back.

He reminded me of an older Samuel L. Jackson with hair and a full beard. Since I joined the band, he was the one person to take me under his wing to help me soar. The former sax player, Fingaz, was a household hit. So I was constantly hazed by the band to make sure I was a good replacement.

Fingaz left because he decided to be a family man and his wife had given birth to their first born. It probably wasn't a good idea for Fingaz to be in the streets of D.C. after nine' o'clock with a newborn depending on him.

"So, you're after Dolly Hunter, eh?" Jupiter asked while opening the back door of the club. We were headed to the alley where our cars were parked.

"Is that her name?"

"Come on man, stop puttin' on like your impromptu set this evening was a coincidence. *Doll's House*, an off the cuff jam? Yeah right!"

"My interest is evident, huh?"

"Sax, the drool is still slidin' out the corner of yo mouth."

"Is it really?" I asked while wiping my mouth with the back of my hand. It very well could be there. Dolly was the object of my affection even if for a few hours. She was eye candy and I wanted to know how sweet her mind and soul would taste.

"I've known Doll for, hmm, let's just say I know her pretty well," Jupiter remarked with a grin.

"What's up with the smirk, Bruh?"

"Doll is an interesting catch. She's a passive predator."

"Explain."

"She looks intimidating. All eyes watching and observing. However, she's just as scared of her prey as they are of her. She's more vulnerable than you think."

"What prey? Is she some kind of black widow or something? 'Cause she didn't seem vulnerable back in the club." I pointed behind me.

"She's more like a house spider. She has a comfort zone and leaves it long enough to be visible. When she's done lookin' 'round she decides whether or not she wants to be seen. Doll will either stick around to build a web or retreat to her hole in the wall never to be seen again. Just know that she's still watching you."

"Oh! She's been hurt in the past and now she's protective of her heart?"

"Exactly! She'll let you in, but just enough to find a fault.

If she likes you, well, she's the type of woman who will give you the world ten times over. Just don't cross her."

"Why didn't you just say that in the first place?" I shook my head.

"Come on, man, you know me. I'm Jupiter."

"Oh, how could I forget?"

"Look, Sax, I think you're a nice guy. So this info is for free. Doll likes to visit Blackplatinum on Friday nights. You might try your luck next week." I nodded. He continued. "Do what you will with the information I gave you. In the meantime, I have a lady in Zion to save in this here spaceship."

I tapped one of his front tires with my right foot. "Yo, man, I think your ship is about to sink. You need some new tires. They're a little burned out."

"Sax," he began while getting in his car, "I always keep fresh rubbas so I won't get burned out. Ya dig?" He winked at me and shut the car door. Jupiter was such a dirty old man. I guess that's how he finds his rhythm on the drums.

"Man, go home to your wife."

Jupiter rolled down the window to give me a pound and we headed our separate ways. His helpful hints on Operation Doll House allowed me to plan my next moves. I'm a writer and a business man. So, it won't be too hard for me to create a way to catch my angel in blue. My persistence alone will get me what I want. If all else fails, my music will send her floating into my arms. Regardless of the outcome, I was willing to take the risk. I just needed to set the reel in motion.

CHAPTER FIVE
Call Waiting

The jam session started at 11pm.
The toast was made at a quarter after the hour.
The glass was filled with strawberry dreams
Drizzling down like rain.
Beaus stand in line
Waiting for a connection.
However, I chose to respond to your call
Without saying a word.

It was two days before my twenty-ninth year on earth——a year away from the big three oh. Thirty used to seem so far away to me. Once it started knocking on my door, I made a concerted effort to stay in shape. On my twenty-fifth birthday, my mom said to me, *Baby, that quarter century mark will show everything you eat. You'd better start toning those blackberry hips before you start looking like you have a kangaroo in your front pouch.* I'm glad I took her advice because it seemed that anything that went into my mouth showed. I swore one day I heard a cow moo when I ate a steak and cheese from a local carry out.

My uncle prepared a special table for my pre-birthday celebration at Blackplatinum. James *Jupiter* Moss, my mother's oldest brother, always looked out for his favorite niece. He told me to wear a red carnation in my hair. I didn't probe any further about his plans. I just had to trust that everything would make sense in the end.

Our table was adorned with a platinum colored tablecloth and sprinkles of metallic purple stars. A tiara and a single rose lay in the chair facing the stage. I assumed that was my special seat. The girls and I were given complimentary glasses of champagne with strawberries capped on the side. I usually pass on drinks but figured, hey, it's my birthday. I can be a bad girl for once.

By the time the band finished the second set I was working on my third glass. I left the Silver Bullet in the garage so the guilt lessened with each sip of what seemed to be heavy consumption of alcohol.

"Look at the ole lady sippin' on her gin and juice," Cita joked.

"You know that's some heavy stuff you're puttin' down, Dawlee?" Erica cosigned.

"Sippin' ain't easy. Besides, I've only had one drink," I lied.

"One?" Cita and Erica exclaimed while rolling their necks.

"Sweetie, these poor strawberries had no chance at gettin' a drink from those glasses of champagne," Erica retorted while dangling the ruby fruit in my face.

I acknowledged my guilt and called the waiter over to bring me a glass of water. The band took a break and I looked around hoping Gerald would get a glimpse of me in my pre-birthday splendor. He was nowhere in sight. My buzz kept me calm for the moment. I started to feel a chill and had to adjust my shawl. A draft was blowing my way.

"I'll get that, Lady," a male's voice offered. I felt the warmth of his hands helping me place the chiffon fabric around my shoulders. I turned in slow motion to greet a beautiful set of pearly whites. It was the famous jazz musician Wynton Marsalis. All I could say was, *Thank you*, while my grin was stuck on pause. Erica and Cita sat with mannequin faces similar to mine.

"I hope we didn't keep you too long," the announcer began on the stage. I wasn't paying too much attention until my name was called. "We have a regular in the house tonight who will be celebrating her birthday on Sunday. To help me pay tribute to Darlene Hunter, I asked Wynton Marsalis to accompany me this evening." I turned around and saw Gerald dressed in a three-pieced, black suit with a red carnation attached to his lapel. Our flowers matched. That Uncle James.

"Darlene, this birthday song is for you." Wynton winked at me as he began his sojourn toward the stage. Blacksax was at it again. Smooth and full of surprises.

"Guurrl!" Erica nudged me with her elbow. This was her way of confirming her approval of Gerald. I smiled inside and out and there was nothing I could do about it.

"The man plays piano and the sax," Cita said with surprise as Gerald took a seat at the baby grand on the stage. "Hmm, you know what that means. Don't you?"

"What, Cita? What does it mean?" I questioned.

"He's good with his hands and his lips!"

"Heeeey!" Cita and Erica exclaimed while toasting to the myth that I hoped was true. I was, however, reluctant to entertain the thought in order to stay focused. My attempt to keep holy thoughts in my head went south for the moment.

The champagne magnified my emotions. How would his piano fingers feel as they outlined the curves of my body? Would his lips be the perfect size to whisper sweet everythings in my ear? I imagined Gerald *Blacksax* Washington exploring what had not been uncovered in years. I had to snap out of it and recognized the reason cranberry juice had to always be my drink of choice. I lack self control under the influence of even the mildest alcoholic beverage. I barely knew the man, but his effort turned me on. My excitement that night...immeasurable. Self-control.

My uncle gave me the thumbs up from the stage. I'm sure he had his hand in the pot that was stewing. I just smirked and shook my head at him in acceptance of his part in my birthday surprise. I then realized that there must be something striking about Gerald besides his looks because Uncle James helped him to get my attention. So, I enjoyed every note played. Blacksax singled me out of all the ladies in the room. He created an atmosphere just for me. I was becoming the hook to his song.

He put a spell on me for the rest of the evening. I didn't even notice that it was 3am and Erica had left Blackplatinum moons ago. Only Cita, myself and a handful of club goers remained in our seats. My eyes were affixed on Gerald. He truly was a melody maker. Before the sun rose from its last few winks of sleep, I decided to let my guard down and open up. Gerald's hard work deserved some compensation. The accounts payable office of my emotions helped me draft a note on the back of my business card. I didn't want to ruin the evening by letting the champagne speak for me. So I inscribed a special message on the card and asked Jimmy to be my mailman once again.

Sax,

The Smithsonian carousel.
Tomorrow. Noon.
Lunch. I'll be there.

-Dolly

CHAPTER SIX
The Knight's Day Trip

Round and round love goes.
Where will it stop?
No one knows.

In hiding, fate will catch you.
In faith, love will keep you.
In the Lord, all that is true will sustain you.

Round and round love goes.
Where will it stop?
No one knows?

A knight
A Lady
A Horse
A Trip
A Lane
In Love
A Risk
I'll Take.

Round and round love goes.
Where will it stop?
Only God knows.

I had to inquire more about Jupiter's insight regarding Dolly. I let him catch some shut-eye that Saturday morning after our chat in the alley. As soon as the lunch whistle sang at noon I blew up his two-way. I may have had four hours of sleep. Half the time I tossed and turned thinking about ways to attract Dolly's attention. She wasn't getting away that easily. Jupiter was my only hope.

He didn't return my page until 5pm. He agreed to meet me at Ben's Chili Bowl. He was already waiting by the time I arrived at six thirty. It was crowded with people getting ready for the next show at the Lincoln Theatre. He stood up to greet me from the dining counter.

"You know I had a honey over, right?"

"Man, please, you're married! Why do you keep fantasizing about your old playa days?"

"Just 'cause I'm married don't mean the lovin' ain't sweet like honey. Besides, Nell made me turn in my playa's card a long time ago. So, I've earned the right to feel like The Mack every once in a while. And a mack I was last night. We had a role play last night and..."

"Alright, playa, spare me the details."

We grabbed one of the empty tables in the back. The walls were covered with newspaper clippings and autographed celebrity pictures. Ben's Chili Bowl's history was told on the four walls of the dining room area. It was one of the few surviving businesses during the riots in the 60s.

"Order what you want, young blood. This meal is on me."

I took advantage of the free meal and ordered two chili

and cheese dogs, chili fries, a Coke, and a slice of pound cake. He ordered the same and then turned to face me.

"How can I help you, Sax?" he asked with a sly grin.

I proceeded to pour my heart out while giving my spiel about my sleep deprivation due to Dolly's compelling beauty.

"Okay, I only know honey as a face in the crowd but Jupe, man, her eyes sparkled and I just know I heard her heart beat. No offense, man, I know you are bad with the sticks but baby girl was bangin' in her outfit. And oooh wee...those slacks she had on with that slit...have mercy! But aside from her being fine and lookin' like the queen of Sosa, I knew she was no ordinary lady, so she was no ordinary song."

While I'm talking, Jupiter continued to laugh at me. I was going bananas over a brown sugar dream whose essence I felt from the stage and through an exchange of cranberry juice in a jazz club. I cut short his laughter with a scowl on my face. Upon seeing how serious I was about my objective to get to know Dolly, Jupiter finally disclosed that she was his favorite niece. How about that? I did, however, find comfort in knowing that he was only being protective. My intentions were, indeed, honorable. I, at the very least, wanted to get one date with her. I couldn't blame Jupiter for being cautious. I would be the same way if I knew some guy was trying to kick it with my sister.

Being a veteran band member, Jupiter had the inside scoop on the celebrity guests coming to town. He informed me that Wynton Marsalis was making an appearance at the club the same weekend as Dolly's birthday. The well-known musician didn't advertise his arrival because he wanted to perform in front of an intimate crowd. Once he determined my interest in

Dolly was true, Jupiter decided to assist me in my quest to get her attention.

The plan:

1. Arrive at Blackplatinum Café early so I could speak with Wynton about assisting me with a birthday tribute to Dolly.

2. Wear a red carnation on my lapel. Jupiter didn't explain why. He told me only that I would understand later.

3. Jupiter said that once I confirmed Wynton's participation he would handle the rest.

I agreed to the plan and prayed it worked. Friday arrived. My staff writers at the magazine noticed my anxiety that morning and suggested that I take the day off. I did. However, as soon as nine thirty rolled around, I rushed out of my townhouse with the smell goods on and hurried to Georgia Avenue. Once at the club, I was a shadow lurking in the dimness of the light. I had a clever idea to reverse roles for a moment and become the spider. I watched Dolly from my comfort zone while a new vocalist entertained the audience for the first half of the evening. I stayed concealed until eleven thirty.

Dolly looked like royalty sitting with her friends. She flirted with my mind even in stillness, even when I was nowhere within her immediate sight. The second hand on my watch seemed to get louder than the band. The tick tock melody mixed with the bass thump of my heart drowned out the close, yet, distant rhythms of the band.

It was eleven twenty-five and thirty seconds when Wynton walked out onto the floor. He looked around and found his target. When he reached Dolly, her back faced him. I could see her smile once she recognized who was attempting to help her with her shawl. She was completely surprised. She looked like a little slice of heaven. She was distracted by Wynton. That was my cue to take the stage.

As soon as I mentioned her name into the microphone, my honey taffy turned around, gazed into my eyes, and I knew I was on my way to getting the girl. I then noticed that she too was wearing a red carnation. Hers was placed in her hair. Jupiter had somehow made us the corny couple you see at amusement parks with matching outfits. Dolly noticed my carnation, touched hers, and smiled shyly. As weird as it may have been for both of us, I welcomed the connection. The night was warm from that moment on. She was sunshine on a cool night. I obviously made an impression because she confirmed our first date on a business card.

Although five hours separated the time I left Blackplatinum and the time I jumped in the shower to get ready for my date with Dolly on the Smithsonian grounds, my heart was operating on daylight savings. Time slowed down in the midst of my excitement. Sleep was not on my list of priorities. I reserved my energy to prepare for an afternoon with a doll.

The Mall was beginning to fill with tourists. Although fall was a few weeks away, they covered the grounds. They left little room for the grass to grow. It was September 11th, three years after the tragic bombing of the World Trade Center and the Pentagon. The only panic on this day was that of a hungry child begging his mother for an overpriced snack combo.

Sitting on the bench, I stared at the carousel only to take my mind off Dolly. I was very anxious to see her. I arrived a few minutes earlier than our scheduled meeting. I didn't want to give Dolly any reason to cancel me out. She made the first move on the chess board of love. I wanted to maintain my position as her knight in training.

"Wow, you're here on time," a voice from behind signaled

me to be aware of my surroundings. It was Dolly. I rose and jumped to my feet to greet her.

"I wanted to make sure I didn't miss you," I said with a smile. "I wouldn't dare have you leave on account of my being late."

"I'm glad to know that you were thinking ahead. I just might enjoy this lunch after all," she giggled.

"Well," I began, "shall we get going?"

Dolly nodded. "Yup. So where are we going to eat?"

"I dunno. You asked me out."

Her face was classic. Mouth open and eyes held wide, Dolly struggled to say, "Uh, I was just responding to your initial request.

I laughed to let her know I was joking and then I grabbed my duffle bag, extended my arm for her to hold, and escorted her to our dining area.

I prepared a picnic for us. The perfect spot was just a stone's throw away from the carousel. I selected a shaded area that gave us a perfect view of the Capitol. I had already spread a red and white blanket under the tree.

"Lunch will be ready in a minute, Ms. Hunter." I removed my arm from hers and motioned for her to take a seat.

"A picnic? How romantic, Mr. Washington."

"I just wanted to give you a taste of what I have to offer under God's sunlight."

Dolly's cutting eyes and curled lip gave me the impression that she didn't believe me. I continued to express my thoughts in hope of convincing her that she wasn't just a pair of thighs I was feeding lies. I placed an assortment of sandwiches on the blanket. She had a choice of ham and American cheese, turkey and Swiss, roast beef and provolone, chicken salad, and tuna salad sandwiches.

"Did you make all this or did Subway deliver this to your home this morning."

"What? A brother can't know his way around the kitchen?" I remarked in shock.

Feeling embarrassed by the questioning of my culinary skills, Dolly lowered her eyes and spoke with meekness.

"I'm not saying you can't cook. It's just that there's a lot of food here and we both left Blackplatinum only a few hours ago."

"I know and you still look delicious."

"Are you flirting with me?" she asked while leaning her head to the side and twirling the ends of her hair.

"Yeah, but that's beside the point. I will admit, Pretty Lady, I did have some help with our lunch. Sarah Lee baked the pie," I hesitated and then said while bowing my head with puppy dog eyes, "and Subway did make the sandwiches."

"Aww," she began with her nurturing voice, "it's the thought that counts." She rubbed my head and smiled a contagious smile.

"So, tell me about yourself," I said while waiting for her to choose a sandwich.

"What do you want to know?"

"What do you want me to know?"

Dolly sighed before answering. "Well, I could tell you that I'm out on parole, but that would just scare you."

"Try me."

"Okay." She shuffled herself close to me and began to whisper while looking around. "You see, I'm a notorious thief. Don't tell anyone, but I steal hearts." "Wow! We have something in common." She wasn't ready for my response. Since she wanted to joke, I joined in the fun.

"Really?" Her eyes grew wide in dismay. "How many can you take in a year?"

"Hmm, let's see," I paused. "My record is pretty low. I'm casing this big job right now. It's kinda tough on the outside but really mushy on the inside. When I pierce through its shell, I'm going to place it right next to mine." Dolly straightened up and was taken aback. She said nonchalantly, "Good luck" and took a bite out of her sandwich.

Passing her a napkin, I said, "Here's my invisible bio. I'm thirty years old, single, no children, and I work hard at everything I do."

"You're a rare species, Mr. Washington."

"I'm almost extinct, Ms. Hunter, but somehow I landed in your city."

"You landed in my city? Don't you live here too?"

"I'm originally from Central Florida. Mickey and I grew up together."

"How did you end up in D.C.?"

"My craft brought me here in search of new talent. I'm a magazine publisher."

"Which magazine do you publish?"

"*Block Writers.*"

"I heard of that magazine. As a matter of fact…I saw one of my kids reading a copy once."

I coughed a little and damn near choked on a piece of lettuce. "One of your kids? How many children came out of that body of yours?"

Dolly's smile was devilish. "I used to teach. I don't have any kids of my own. I did treat my students as if I birthed them. Now I'm in real estate tryin' to close on that million dollar house in Potomac," she sang her last words and snapped her fingers in the air in excitement.

"Now I see why you couldn't have lunch with me last weekend. Busy showin' houses, eh?"

"Yup!. By the way, you owe me. I missed out on three appointments to be here with you."

"I hope it was worth the trouble."

"That remains to be seen, Blaaacksaaax." She exaggerated my stage name.

Through her discourse about her students and real estate ventures, I could see Dolly's loving personality. She smiled from ear to ear when talking about her past and current careers.

"Ever been married, Dolly?"

"Almost and with that said, I have to be convinced out of the single life. So, Mr. Washington, I am also on the endangered species list of WPWF."

"WPWF?"

"I'm a Working Professional Without a Family." She was pretty clever with the acronym. I liked her sense of humor.

"Although endangered, I bet you're a great catch."

"Well, I don't mind being caught. It's the poaching that bothers me."

"Understood, Lady. Understood."

The ice was broken. Our afternoon lunch was a winner but it was up to me to make sure she agreed to see me again. God's sunshine reflecting on Dolly's face was a thumbs up from above. I just needed to remain in the right posture to allow her the freedom to be herself. I was convinced that I was the knight this lady needed to ride on love's carousel. I could write a million scores for her. She was becoming my new melody.

CHAPTER SEVEN
Vivaciously Exhilarating

In my threshold is a solemn promise of truth and friendship
Although roots from your Southern palace take a detour to
my throne,
There's always the sweet taste of mango seeping through my
veins.

The strength of my tree and
The thickness of my roots
May catch you in the rapture of the forest.
Evergreens blowing in the wind, my hair flows
Black as the night that covers me, you, us,
You still smell my spice yet tasting the sweet of my
threshold.

I feel beautiful as I walk through life's snow
That falls on my brown skin.
I turn into a glass of chocolate milk but warm enough to be
a cup of mocha Cappuccino or a handful of coffee dreams.
Will repetition of your song leave my lips? Your song? My
lips?
Or
Will the refrain from my tune play effortlessly in your head
thus creating the
Masterpiece
Preceding this classical score?

*The golden rules of this role we play are encrypted in a
capsule unseen to others
The key and the lock are examples of inertia but not too
soon before Newton's apple makes its journey.
Gravity holds that key in its place while the lock is
apprehensive to make a way for entry.*

*I am laughing like a hyena after its prey.
Only the smile is not of deception
But sincerity.*

*So I thank you for that afternoon joy you put in my heart.
I challenge you to seek that Evergreen forest for a missing
leaf
That makes me vivaciously exhilarating.*

The romantic setting was one of the highlights of our first date. The birds sang the prelude to our afternoon. Their chirps and whistles made for a great soundtrack to our reality screenplay.

At high noon, the sun was perfectly positioned between the leaves of the tree where we sat. We took center stage on the grounds of the Smithsonian. Gerald was kind. He even wiped the mayonnaise from my sandwich that took residence on the corner of my lip. He turned something so embarrassing into something quite endearing. I really enjoyed the gentle touch from his fingertips as he held my hand when I spoke. They felt exactly as I imagined. They were strong and warm.

I was quite impressed because he was very attentive after asking me about my college experience. Whenever I discussed my alma mater, I left little room for questions. I bleed blue and white.

"You're an educated woman, Dolly."

"And how do you know that?"

"Your presence exudes institution of higher learning."

"Well, yes, I believe you're right."

"Tell me about your undergraduate experience. Why did you choose...?"

"Hampton?" My eyes lit up.

Hampton was a topic I loved to discuss. I told Gerald about the college tour Cita, Erica, and I went on during our junior year of high school. The tour was during the spring. Hampton was the first school on the bus route. Of all the schools in the south, I gravitated towards my *Home by the Sea*.

Everything about the school was collegiate. The setting

was perfect for a learning environment. It was set right on the water. Ducks were scattered along the riverbank while students were studying on benches under several of the trees planted around the yard. The chapel bell rang every hour just like a scene in the movies depicting college life. The fraternity and sorority members stepped for us during our welcome ceremony. Although I never joined any of the sisterhoods, I always marveled at the camaraderie between the Black Greek Letter Organizations. The Argh Argh from the Omegas and the OO-OOP from the Deltas could be heard from several feet away. I loved the call and response.

We were scheduled to visit other black colleges: Fayetteville State, Winston Salem, and North Carolina A & T. Erica and I both grabbed applications for admission to Hampton and filled them out on the way to our next stop. Erica's motivation was different from mine. She loved the quality of men on the campus. I was attracted to the scenery and the strong sense of family. The course offerings were excellent, but even more I knew I would be able to achieve a higher level of success when I knew the faculty and my peers were behind me academically, emotionally, and spiritually. Hampton became my home for four years.

After lunch, Gerald and I walked around the Museum of Natural History. I wanted to check out the geology section. I am a big fan of gems. The first exhibit contained the Hope Diamond. It's similar to the fictitious Heart of the Ocean mentioned in the movie *Titanic* but much more beautiful and real.

"Is this the kinda rock you're expecting your fiancé to buy you, Miss Dolly?"

"I don't think I could handle forty-five point five carats.

Besides, I don't want to be responsible for something that's a trillion years old."

"And the fact that it has a curse attached to it would scare you away, too."

"So, you know a little something, eh?"

"I'm not just some musician trying to catch a beat. Legend says that whoever is in possession of it suffers many troubles." I shook my head in approval and he rubbed his goatee and said, "I'm well read, Lady."

"Okay. Then, what was the original weight of the diamond?" I folded my arms and waited for a response.

Gerald moved toward me and pulled my hand close to his heart while slowly whispering in my left ear, "The original weight of the Hope Diamond was one hundred twelve and three sixteenths carats."

Gerald's voice was a drum inside my soul and his breath was as fresh as the mint of the Altoid he placed in his mouth after our meal. However, there was certainly something fishy about the way he responded. I turned from his embrace and looked behind me.

"You cheated!" I exclaimed as I hit him on the arm for looking at the history of the Hope Diamond affixed to the wall just behind me.

Gerald laughed, "I told you I could read." I couldn't blame him for using his brain. I certainly couldn't be angry with a man whose bottom lip was juicier than a orange slice.

We held hands throughout our visit on The Mall. Gerald asked me why I was still single. I told him I was waiting on the man God created for me. He stared at me with conviction as if to tell me something. I couldn't help but stare back.

Aside from being a victim in love, I wasn't always the most innocent in relationships. My first two years of college I dated often. On any given weekend, I exploited the idea that I was in college and that appeared to be quite attractive to the locals at Hampton. My motto: *Free Food Never Hurt Nobody.* The fact that I didn't spread legs easily for the spoils became a little problem for some of the guys financing my meals. Gerald said we had more in common than I realized. He traded company for home cooked meals. He did admit, however, that his self-control did not match mine.

"It's kinda hard to say no when it's in your face. But I'm saved now," he professed while mimicking the church ladies waving their hands in the air. He told me he'd tell me some other time about the leash that slowed his roll.

I got boogie with a few brothers, but I chose my *fun buddies* carefully. My excuse was to relieve the pressures of term papers and tests. I never hooked up with anyone on campus because it was too small. I couldn't have my business on the yard. Newport News and Norfolk were neighboring cities in Hampton. I dated guys who lived on the outskirts of school, locals with benefits. I tried not to get attached because I knew I was headed back home after graduation. The Tidewater area was a place you come back to for homecoming and once you've accomplished all your goals and retired. Gerald got a kick out of my abridged version of my college days.

We left the geology section and went to the cafeteria. Gerald had a craving for sweets. He bought two ice cream sandwiches for us and then came up with the bright idea to have a scavenger hunt. He enjoyed competition and the thrill of the hunt. He was able to find all the exhibits much faster than I did. Hmm. Perhaps he scoped out the museum prior to our meeting. After all, it was his idea.

Although I felt completely comfortable in his presence, I had to be like a sleeping cat with one eye open. Cita and

Erica tried to convince me to simply enjoy myself with Gerald. One part of me stood firm on being careful with my heart and risk the chance of losing him rather than losing myself in the process. The other part of me was pressing me to take the chance and simply allow myself the pleasure of the ride. The arrogant side of me remarked, *If it's meant to be, he wouldn't mind the chase.*

Maybe I was afraid the climax of my story involving Gerald would end before it had a chance to blossom. Maybe being with Gerald could somehow mend the roots once broken from my tree of life. Then again, there was so much chaos around my foliage that it really was hard to see the forest for the trees. I only hoped his shovel was big enough to dig around my weeds before I turned into a self-absorbed mushroom.

I updated Erica and Cita on my Saturday afternoon with Gerald as we walked into the bridal boutique. Our first three attempts to pick out dresses for Erica's wedding was a bust. So, we were back again for a fourth time.

"He wants to take me out for my birthday tonight."

"Uh huh," Cita remarked. "Whatcha gone do?"

"I told him I'd call him. Are these the dresses, Erica?"

"Stop evading and answer the question," Cita sharply attacked while sucking her teeth. I bowed my head. "I don't know what to do with you. Playing with that man's emotions doesn't make nary bit of sense. You're probably gonna stand him up. Aren't you?" Erica and Cita shook their heads in dismay.

"You ought to know better after everything that's happened to you, Darlene Michelle Hunter."

I knew Erica was frustrated because she called me by my full name. She snatched a selection of lavender satin dresses off the rack and guided us to the dressing room.

"Let your conscience be your guide. We're as close to

biological sisters as you're gonna have and we know a good man when we see one, chile."

"You know as much about him as I do, Cita."

"That may be true, but trust me, the eyes don't lie."

Erica cosigned, "Cita's right, Dawlee, the last guy you thought was *the one* was clearly an asshole. We knew it and told you so. Now Gerald, we can tell…"

"You can tell what?" I interjected with widened eyes.

"We can tell that Sax seems sincere, Doll. He had that school boy crush glow when talking to you outside Blackplatinum."

"Oh Dawlee, I could spend forever in your eyes," Erica teased.

"He didn't say that!"

"I know…but he wanted to. Gimme some gurl!" Cita and Erica slapped high fives while laughing.

"He could be a DL brutha, though. But that ain't nuthin' new." Cita signaled Erica to be quiet because she was about to open a can of worms none of us really wanted to digest.

I once liked a guy in my real estate class who later opened up to me about his sexuality. We had lunch a few times and just when I thought he was being a gentleman by not making advances toward me, he confessed that he had stopped desiring women years ago. He was oh so fine with chiseled arms and God knows what else. I appreciated his honesty, but talk about a self-esteem buster. We remained friends and he often helped me with some high profile clients.

"Look, I just want to be careful. I don't want to get my hopes up and he turns out to be another rascal who wasted my time. Now, I went out with him once and that should be enough. Right?" There was silence.

"Hello?" I was looking for someone to agree with me.

"Yeah. Whatever. All I'm sayin', is that you have to give true love a try."

"Easy for you to say Miss I'm Getting Married."

"Well, I ain't gettin' married, yet, so I can speak on it. We'll be here when your tears fall. If they're tears of joy, we'll cry with ya. If they're tears of sadness, we'll still cry wit ya. But I'll be damned if you'll consume yourself with work, thirty years go by and you're at home with a house full of cats and Medicaid. 'Cause ya ain't sleepin' in the bed with me and mine." Erica exclaimed!

"Hello!" Cita and Erica slapped hands.

"See, that's ya'lls problem. I don't need a man to define me."

"But he can sho keep ya warma and wetta than a cat. Unless you're one of those freaky deakies."

Gerald was attractive, nice, and seemed to give off a good spirit. In trying to weigh the pros and cons of going out with him again, I could only think of reasons why I should. He was on time for our lunch. Pro. I was surprised by the picnic on the Mall. Pro. It was a sweet gesture especially since we had just left the club a few hours before meeting. He was innovative. Pro. He said he was saved. Pro. What was the problem?

While cramming my hips into the skirt of a two-piece formal, I continued to daydream about the possibilities of going out with Gerald again. Cita and Erica were attempting to pull out the Vaseline to help me into the garment. I was able to keep my body toned with the exception of my hips. I inherited them from the Moss side of the family. I really was an hourglass.

"Hmm, gurl, you might wanna jump on the phone with Gerald before you gain another inch on these hips." Cita tapped my thighs with a hanger.

"Give her a break and let's just look for another size."

"Actually, can we get a one-piece? I think even if I could fit the next size up, I'll look crazy. I'm shaped like a pear." I turned in the mirror to look at my body.

"Although it's my wedding, we can get another style on one condition." Cita and I looked at Erica with inquisitive eyes as she reached into her purse. She pulled out her cell phone.

"Call the man!"

I rolled my eyes at Erica. In the back of my mind, I really thought, *What the hell.* I retrieved Gerald's phone number from my organizer and called.

"Hello, may I speak to Gerald?"

CHAPTER EIGHT
Fire and Water

What makes the hot air cool?
A splash in the pool as the night falls on your body?
A sizzling delight comes on board as fire and water create
steam.
Can you feel it?
Sweat drips effortlessly down your back as I cup my hands
to catch your excitement personified.
Calming the raging river that crashes
Against the solid rock,
I'll kiss the spot on your neck,
The nape or the small of your back..
I'll move toward your aching lumbar
To provide relief from the vertebrae once bent by vindictive
storms.
What makes the hot air cool?
A splash in the pool as the knight falls on your body.

Dolly called and accepted my invitation to take her out for her birthday. I tried to remain as smooth as the notes played on my saxophone. However, if Dolly had been a fly on the wall, she would have seen me cheesing from ear to ear.

I told her to wear something comfortable and light for our date. My mission? It was my intent to send Dolly floating on a bed of clouds. Whatever shell surrounded her heart was going to be shattered and she was going to experience a relaxing birthday.

Just as the sun was setting, I pulled up to her townhouse. It was located in a quaint neighborhood in Upper Marlboro, Maryland. The city girl moved to the suburbs. It was right off Route 214, a few miles up the road from the stadium where the Redskins play. If things worked out, I could catch a game at FedEx Field and then drive to her house for a late afternoon dinner. This is all assuming the woman could cook.

My daydream of Dolly in a kitchen with sweatpants and a tank top on frying chicken was interrupted by the sound of her miniature neighbor.

"Hi! Do you live around here?" A little girl who appeared to be close to six years old stood before me with cowry shells dangling from the ends of her braided hair.

I laughed and bent to her level. "No, baby girl, I don't. I'm coming to visit a friend."

"My mommy is looking for someone to go out with. Can you be her friend?" She smiled showing few teeth and exposed gums. I presumed that the tooth fairy had her bottom and top fronts. I was shocked by the little girl's aggressiveness. Yet, I returned the smile and told her that I could only handle one friend at a time. I gave her a pat on the head and started walking to Dolly's house.

I climbed the stairs to thirty-eight Harry S. Truman Lane and rang the doorbell. It played the tune of *Happy Birthday*. As she opened the door, a whiff of her perfume danced across my nose. Bouncing back into reality, I greeted her.

"Hello, birthday girl," I said while handing Dolly a dozen purple tulips. Her eyes were glowing fireworks.

"Wow! How did you know my favorite color is purple... and...and...that I love tulips?"

"I pay attention. Besides, the picture on your organizer gave me a hint." I received a half-cornered smile. Then I asked, "May I come in or shall I wait for you on the steps?"

Just as I presumptuously took a step toward the inside of her home, Dolly winked at me and said, "Wait here." She took the flowers, thanked me, closed the door and left me standing on her porch.

I sat at her doorstep and the little girl from the parking lot found a home next to me with a pen and a notepad.

"So what's your name? Where do you live? And what's your sign?"

I was hesitant to respond. You'd think with increased violence parents would teach their children not to talk to strangers. Before I could open my mouth to respond, an older woman wearing a house coat, slippers, and pink rollers rescued me from the budding journalist.

"Mista, I'm sawry. My grandbaby is always tryin' ta find a husband for my daughter. Come on here, Ranika." She grabbed the child by the ear. The girl's scream was so loud that half the neighborhood could hear her tantrum until Grandma closed the door to their home.

"Ready?" Dolly popped out of her door.

"For a minute I thought I was gonna have to take Ranika up on her offer."

"Ranika?" Dolly peered around to try and figure out what I was talking about. She quickly became unconcerned and shrugged her shoulders. "Anyway, I was ready. I was just being anal."

"And if I had left?"

"Then you would have missed out on having a fabulous date with me." Dolly brushed her shoulders off and bumped me with her hip nearly knocking me down two steps.

I extended my hand for her to follow. She accepted it like a kid in a candy store.

"So, where's my horse and carriage?" Dolly asked jokingly.

I pointed to my black, Kawasaki. Her eyes lit up.

"I told you to wear something light and comfortable," I replied while motioning her toward the back of my bike.

I know she saw the saliva coming out of my mouth while I peeked at the firmness of her apple bottom. Dolly was no Barbie doll. She had plenty to hold on to when the weather got cool. Everything about her hips and thighs screamed black woman. I'm glad my bike was big enough to handle her curves. Her red v-neck top properly accentuated her torso. A handful of loving was all I needed in the summer, winter, spring, and fall. She wore a soft leather jacket to take the chill off her arms. I would have gladly been the animal who died to be wrapped around her skin.

"Hold on, Lady." I handed Dolly a helmet and placed mine over my head.

I hopped on the bike and turned on the engine. As we pulled out of Dolly's development, I waved to Ranika. She was watching from a window. When I stopped at the red light, I took one more look at my black beauty before riding her off into the sunset. She smiled at me and I knew the rest of the date was going to be all right. She squeezed my waist and I placed my hand over hers. Dolly was my fire and I was the water to tame her energy for a new course.

CHAPTER NINE
Getting Over the Bridge

"We'll cross that bridge when we get there,"
My mother would say
On a day when trouble seemed to lurk.
Somehow, the waters aren't crashing this time
And the current is singing a song of promise
The coal I thought was there
Was turning into a sparkling diamond.
I'm crossing the bridge and seeing a new light
Troubles don't last forever.

Ｈow dare Gerald show up on my doorstep looking like a fudge sickle? I was ready to eat him up. Didn't he know a black man in a black leather jacket riding a black motorcycle was my weakness? I tried to ignore his advances but the smell of his cologne traveling from him to my nose, to my brain, made me powerless. He wore a classic scent that never grows old, Obsession.

I did enjoy the ride. The more Gerald accelerated, the tighter I held him. My body tingled each time he acknowledged my touch by placing his hand over mine.

I don't know if I was hot and bothered or if it was the thrill of being on the back of his bike, but somehow the thought of Gerald excited me and there was nothing I could do about it. It was my birthday and I could enjoy my fantasy. I was a biker girl riding into the sunset with a fine man. Although I didn't want to completely admit it to myself at first, I actually wanted to relish in the moment with a man without plotting my next steps to get rid of him. I was having fun. Erica and Cita would be proud.

I failed to ask about our destination. I did know, however, it was somewhere north because Gerald took I495 toward Baltimore. The air was crisp and there was no precipitation. I found myself getting lost in the scenery. Although it was familiar territory as I've traveled the beltway on too many occasions getting back and forth to the mall, there was something new about it. I took the time to appreciate the fresh smell of the leaves and grass. The trees were gigantic stories of the past. They spoke to me saying, *We've withstood the storm and conquered the winds. No matter what elements come our way, the choice to stand and to be strong is our mission.* What a testimony.

Gerald exited at Route 50 headed toward Annapolis. My hopes of having dinner at the Inner Harbor blew away into the wind. Exit 22. Riva Road was a memory, so Macaroni Grill was out of the plan. Then, I became concerned when I saw the signs for the Bay Bridge.

"Hey, biker boy, where are we going?"

"Huh?"

"Pull over!" I yelled.

Gerald maneuvered the bike toward the emergency lane, stopped, and turned off the engine. We both took off our helmets and stepped onto the pavement.

"What's up baby?"

Baby? Wow. I was promoted from Dolly to Baby. Okay. The violins stopped for a moment. I was worried about my safety.

"This is nice and all, you know, riding the bike and such, but…"

"But what? Do you think I'm driving you to some remote place to chop you into little pieces and sell you on the black market?" Gerald laughed after his response. I didn't find his humor too funny. I punched his shoulder.

"Stop playing. Where are we going?"

Gerald came closer to me while running his hands through my hair. "To an oasis from the rest of the world."

I removed his hand. His touch felt great, but I had to be focused. "You'd better tell me where we're going before I whoop your oasis."

"Alright! Alright!" Gerald said while backing away from me. "I'm taking you to a little spot just up the way."

A vague answer. Men. Why can't he just be straight up?

"I'm not going to do any harm to you. I just want you to enjoy a special moment on your special day."

I looked at Gerald with skeptical eyes. Then I realized I had mace in my handbag and decided to go along with the plan. I hopped back on the bike. He smiled and we were off once again.

I watched the sky change colors as we crossed the 4.3 mile Bay Bridge. Slivers of blue were scattered throughout the reddish-orange mirage. Flying birds were a perfect contrast to the fall sky. They flew in the shape of the letter V. The ripples in the water looked like small dolphins synchronized to a silent rhythm. My anxiety turned to excitement. If Gerald's surprise was as nice as the ride, I had no reason to worry. My body felt so good against his. I couldn't resist the opportunity to squeeze him like a teddy bear. I felt a bulge through his coat. He worked out and that was good stuff.

Gerald pulled into a marina. Many of the yachts were decorated with lights. He parked the bike, helped me down, and led the way. Just beyond the entrance was a sign for Marina Bay Seafood. The restaurant was so inconspicuous. It looked like the other yachts docked in the marina only a lot bigger. It was the dinner cruise that never left the dock.

"I'm allergic to seafood, Gerald." I remarked. His face looked flushed.

"Really?"

"No," I replied with a chuckle. "I was just playing around," I giggled.

Once we approached the entrance, Gerald jumped ahead of me to show his chivalry. He opened the door. We were greeted by a line of six hosts. There were three on the left and three on the right side. We walked along an ocean blue carpet. Tropical fish swam in the tanks on each side of the wall.

"Welcome to Marina Bay," the hosts exclaimed with glee. They wore tuxedos.

"Reservations for G. Washington," Gerald said to the Maitre'd. The reservation list was skimmed and we were escorted to our table. We were seated at a table for two on the heated deck. We had a great view of the water. We were literally sitting on the dock of the bay.

"Your waiter will be with you in a moment." The host placed the menus on the table.

"Nice pick, Mr. Washington," I said while perusing the a lá carte menu.

"Nothing's too nice for you, Darlene Hunter."

"I would have worn something more elegant like my diamonds and pearls.

"Prince fan?" he asked.

"Who isn't?"

"Well, you look fine the way you are." He grabbed my hand and like chocolate on concrete during the heat of summer, the melting of my heart started again. He cleared his throat and quickly resumed an upright position. It was obvious that he felt the energy between us too.

"So what did you do for your birthday?"

"Well, I got up and went to early service. When I returned to the house, my girls surprised me with a birthday cake."

"You all live together?

"No. They just have the spare keys to my house in case of an emergency."

He kissed my hand. "Continue."

"There's really nothing else to tell accept that my uncle and auntie came over to bring me some new tulip bulbs to plant. They give me a dozen each year since I bought the house. The tulips are reminders that everything and everyone has a season.

We bloom best when it's our time. I never know the color until around Easter. So even if I have a bad winter, I always have something to look forward to in the spring. Besides that, I returned some messages, took a nap, and now I'm here."

"Sounds like a peaceful birthday to me."

"It really was."

"Did you talk to your parents?" Nice segue to get me to talk about my family.

"Yeah, they called me from some cabin in the mountains. They sent me a really nice painting from an art gallery in New York City."

"I'd love to see it some time."

"That would require you to step over my threshold."

"Only by invitation."

"You think I should extend one?."

"Of course," he said with confidence while folding his napkin on his lap to prepare for the breaking of bread. I placed my napkin on my lap as well.

The waiter took our drink orders. I allowed Gerald to order for me. He requested a cranberry juice for me and hot tea for himself. He said he felt a sore throat coming on. I instantly thought *there goes our first kiss.* I quickly dismissed the notion and just continued to enjoy the conversation.

"You know," I started while buttering a sesame roll, "I was thinking about something you said during our picnic on the Mall."

"What's that?" Gerald looked puzzled as he broke his hard roll in half.

"Do you remember saying that you wanted to give me a taste of what you have to offer under God's sunlight?"

"I sure do."

Without sounding like I was Miss Holier Than Thou, I

asked, "Well, what exactly do you know about God? Inquiring minds want to know." I used my facial muscles to force my eyebrows to do the Bankhead Bounce.

He paused, smiled, and replied, "I know that the next woman I make my Special Lady must be prepared to get on her knees and fight demons with me through prayer and scripture."

I was simmered, seared, and done. I needed no further confirmation that I would continue my quest and dig deeper into the life of Mr. Washington. A man seeking a woman to be his spiritual partner. There was a lot to be said about that. Most men just want a woman to get on her knees to confirm his manhood, not to show that her strength comes through prayer. I liked Gerald's thought pattern. I relaxed even more. I was in good hands.

We were ready to place our order. Gerald flagged down the waiter. Coincidently, we both wanted the steak and salmon entrée with rice pilaf and seasoned vegetables. Gerald added two baked potatoes to his meal. He made it known that he loved starches. I told him those starches would catch up to him without exercise. I was quickly made aware of his four-time a week workout regimen and he then invited me to jog with him when I was ready to put my feet on the concrete. I was cautioned not to work off too much because like many men, he desired the cushion that makes a woman's body feminine.

"Bones is a game of dominos, Dolly. I like my woman to have a little squeeze on her." He pinched my arm gently. I squirmed away but slow enough to show him I liked his touch but quick enough to act like it hurt.

The conversation was on its way to a sauna, heated. I changed the subject to let his loins cool and to start building a dam for Lady Sunshine as well. There was something sexy about a man working out and building up his stamina that made my pastor's sermons sound like the teacher from Charlie Brown. I had to be focused. This was only our second date.

"Tell me about your family, Gerald."

"Both my parents are still alive and healthy in Florida. I have a younger sister and two older brothers."

"Musta been difficult growing up with a bunch of hard heads."

"She managed."

"Are your brothers as fine as you?"

"You think I'm fine, eh?"

"Answer the question, silly."

"They're good looking, but both are married with kids. So you can't get with 'em."

"Aw man." I snapped my fingers in playful disappointment.

"My family is pretty close," Gerald admitted.

"Mine too."

"Big too."

"We're still talking about your family, right?" I questioned with playful suspicion.

"Depends...," he remarked moving his hand closer to mine.

"I'm just being bad, continue."

"Naw, Dolly, don't act innocent now. I'm tellin' ya uncle."

"Tell 'em, I don't care," I curled up my lips and rolled my eyes.

"Okay," Gerald shrugged his shoulders and reached for his cell phone. I swiftly stopped him and told him I was just playing.

"That's what I thought! So, anyway, as I was saying before I was interrupted with somebody's nasty thoughts," he widened his eyes in my direction. "My family had a fit when I decided to leave the sunshine state. I broke away from the pack in search of a dream. I wanted to do something different."

"What do you mean?"

"Dolly, you have to understand that Florida is a wonderful place, but it's not a place to make money. It's where you go after you've accumulated wealth and settle down."

"Seems like the quality of life would be great if you just live a simple life."

"Simple life, yes, but I want to build capital on my own."

"What do your parents do?"

"My mother was a cook and my father is a retired postal worker for Polk County. My family isn't hurting but I want to create a new legacy.

"A new legacy?"

"I'll explain when the time is right."

"Well, it seems like your parents did a pretty good job of raising you off their pay."

"Yeah. You're right. I admire the hard work they put in to keep the family together. Again, the Washingtons aren't hurting." He gave me a wink.

"Are your parents your role models?" My curiosity was rising. I wanted to know if Gerald came from good stock. If not, we'd have to work around that.

"Indeed they are. I want to love my wife as much as my father loves my mother. I want to be a fantastic father and rear my sons—"

"Or daughters," I interjected.

"Or daughters...to be the best and brightest stars they can be." Gerald's face turned proud like a bird who just saw its offspring fly for the first time.

"Very interesting, Mr. Washington. Very interesting."

"So what about your family?"

"What would you like to know?" I asked.

"Whatever you're willing to tell me, Lady."

My parents retired from the government and moved to Upstate New York after I finished Hampton. They come out of their love shack only for big occasions. I could count on seeing them at the family reunion during Thanksgiving in North Carolina. Weldon was where my parents met and most of our family lived. I had several aunts, uncles, and cousins who never left North Carolina. My parents, Uncle James, and a number of other family members migrated to many different regions of the country for economic reasons, just like Gerald.

For Christmas, Ma and Daddy usually traveled to some island. As I got older, our communication was mostly through email and phone calls. I was so happy when I got unlimited long distance on my land line because they were costing me a mint. I sometimes wondered whether they would come down when I gave birth to my first child if I delivered on a date not scheduled for a wedding or funeral. Just in case, I considered planning my pregnancy around their schedule. Nonetheless, I loved them and they loved me. When telling Gerald this, he brought comfort to my pessimistic thoughts and told me not to worry about it.

"Although I haven't met your parents, I'm sure they'll be the next ones rushing to your hospital room after me," he chuckled after that subliminal message. I didn't refute it. It was rather nice of him to consider me in that way.

Just when dinner arrived, Gerald questioned me about my siblings. The older brother I did have died in a car accident a few weeks after he finished graduate school. I rarely talked about Ricky. I guess I never truly dealt with the loss of my best friend and hero. I sort of developed a false growth in terms of getting through his death. By no means did this mean I didn't care. I just had to deal with the situation in my own way.

I pulled out the one picture of Ricky and I that reminded me of happier days with him. My glasses fell out my purse while retrieving the photograph. Gerald jokingly called me *four eyes* just before telling me that my brother and I looked like two best friends. We were.

We continued to talk through dinner. The other patrons stared at us as we sang songs by Troop, Frankie Beverly, New Edition, and other old school jams from our youth. Gerald and I tried to discuss the psychology behind the game *It* and just discovered when black folks can't afford to buy games, we just make up entertainment and have fun at minimal cost.

After dinner, Gerald had the wait staff bring a slice of chocolate cake with a candle on it. Rather than make a scene with a crowd of strangers encircled around me in song, Gerald opted to sing Happy Birthday to me and kissed me on the cheek. It was sweet. The cake and the kiss. I thanked him with a return kiss on the cheek.

Gerald paid the bill but we didn't leave the restaurant. Our conversation was so engaging. The noise in the atmosphere was seemingly placed on mute. I could see his eyes and lips moving to a rhythm only I could hear. It was to the beat of my new heart. My tape of bad relationships was erased. God was recording new footage, uncut and in raw form. The director called action and I gladly stepped into place. Act 1. Scene 1.

CHAPTER TEN
Perfect 10

On a scale of one to fifteen
I deducted 5 points to make her my perfect 10
Two points for her smile
Two points for personality
Two points for her style
Two points for spirituality
Two points for accepting my offer
Minus five for not coming into my life sooner.
She is my A plus queen preparing to take her throne.

I became the wax of a candle on a rug. It was hard to remove my attention from Ms. Hunter. I took pleasure in being around Dolly. She asked the right questions and I loved answering them. Dolly made me melt when she asked about my walk with God. She spoke of her love for children and her hope that one day she would be able to play her role as wife and mother under the direction of her husband who was under the direction of God. Until then, she planned to continue worshipping and accepting her singleness as a gift until she became a present waiting to be unwrapped.

Since moving to D.C., the women have been more interested in how much money I have, what kind of car I drive, and what kind of motor is in my pants. There's nothing wrong with making sure I'm self-sufficient and out of my mama's house. However, I've found that some women only base their criteria on monetary and tangible things. Superficial. I realized during dinner at Marina Bay that Dolly was just as beautiful internally as she was externally. She was the difference between a pretty woman and a beautiful woman. Her tough girl act was just that, an act. Inside, she was sweeter than Mama's tea on a spring day.

I invited her for a walk around the marina to let our dinner digest before getting back on the bike. It was chilly but I assured her that the conversation would be inviting enough to keep her warm.

"I enjoyed dinner tonight," she said.

"Good," I replied smiling.

"And the bike ride."

"Good."

Then she stopped, turned to face me, and said, "And I loved that you took the time to find purple tulips to make me smile."

I started to sing to the tune of a Ralph Tresvant song, "I had to do what I had to do to win your heart."

"Aaww shucks! Sang that song, nah!"

"Come on now, you know I can. I'm a musician."

"That don't mean you can saaang!"

"I didn't hear any objections when I had you in the palm of my hands serenading you with a birthday song."

"I just didn't want to embarrass you."

"Okay. We'll see who I play for next week at the club." Dolly gave me the *I wish you would* look. I quickly told her I was just playing around.

"Brrrrr." The cold air was biting Dolly. I rubbed her shoulders and arms with my hands. She had on her leather jacket and I had on my leather gloves to create warm friction. I assumed it helped because she started talking smack again.

"You couldn't pick me up in a car, eh? Tell the truth, you don't have one."

"Aw, gurl, you got me."

"Let me find out you're a hot bamma."

"Bamma? I'm from Florida."

"Not a bamma as in you're from Alabama. A bamma as in a square."

"Oh."

"We got a lotta work to do."

"I'm willing to learn if you're the teacher in the mini skirt and heel at the front of the class."

"You'd betta go ahead with that Mr. Walk A Mile instead of driving."

"I was just playing with you. I have a car, woman. I just

know how you D.C. women like bad boys on bikes. I'll pick you up in the Geo next time."

"You have a Geo?" she asked with bewilderment.

"Yeah! What's wrong with that? I took out the bucket seats and installed custom ones."

"Oh boy!" She turned around while rolling her eyes. "You're a bigger bamma than I thought. But you're cute. So, I'll let you slide."

"Lady, I'm just playing. I ain't got no Geo."

"*I ain't got no Geo.*" Dolly mimicked me in a deep, yet feminine voice. "Who was your English teacher?"

"Hey, I'm not on the clock right now, baby. I'm chillin'." I reached for her arm and pulled her closer to me. The draft from the water was making the hawk come out.

"Seriously Darlene," I looked into her almond shaped eyes while speaking, "I like you. I like you a lot. You're smart, you're funny, and you seem to be pretty..."

"Oh thank you. I try to keep up with my appearance."

"Woman! Would you stop cutting me off?" I laughed to show her I was half joking and half serious. "Anyway, you seem to be pretty well grounded in your career and spirit."

"Gerald, it's so early in the game. You might decide in a few weeks you don't like me."

"Baby girl, I told you I don't play games. And anyway, if I see something I like, I go after it. We Washington men have a pretty good judgment about the company we keep. It's in our genes. The men in my family see the woman they want and it becomes a mission to make her a Washington.

"You think I could be a Washington?"

"If you act right."

"Please! If you act right I might make you a Hunter."

"I've done my share of shopping around, sweets."

"You're not buying a pair of shoes, Gerald."

"Well, if I was buying a pair of shoes and you're the last size 12 in the store, I want to take you home before someone else gets their hands on you."

She seemed to have heard this dialogue one too many times. Expecting that, I knew I had to separate myself from other men before giving her a reason to retreat into her safe haven.

"I don't know where our path will lead us, but I don't want to miss the opportunity to find out. I want to keep hanging out with you."

"So, how do you suppose we'll do that?"

"I'd like to date you as often as you'll allow. You know, get to know what makes you smile, what upsets you, and anything else you'd let me explore."

"Explore? Do I look like National Geographic?" she laughed.

I cupped her chin and replied, "No. I just want to understand what makes Darlene Hunter the darling Dolly I'm getting to know."

"Well, Gerald, I admit, your compliments make it hard for me to turn down your offer."

"Then don't."

"Let me check my calendar." She began to look in her purse before I stopped her.

"No, Lady, check your heart 'cause I'm serious about my intentions. I want to see you again."

I was letting my heart speak and be heard through my mouth. I just wrote a check so my ass ('scuse me Lord) had to be ready to cash it because a woman like Dolly doesn't have time for insufficient funds. I began to tell Dolly the substance behind my words. It was clear to me that I wanted Dolly to know the Gerald of old in order to convince her to give the Gerald she knew a chance to take her off the market.

It was getting too cold to have Dolly standing out by the water. We headed back to her house. It was still pretty early and the second half of the game was on. I was glad to know I could chill and watch football with Dolly. She could follow it really well for a woman, no insult intended. It's a guy thing. We were building. We were so comfortable with each other that I knew I would enjoy our friendship and ultimately that a great relationship.

"We should do this on a regular." I said during the commercial break.

"Oh yeah? The next game is at your house. You're not gonna lay up on my couch every Sunday."

"That's a bet, Lady."

After the game, we had a long chat about my past. Dolly reminded me that I had to break it down to the barest of bones. I didn't hesitate to go into detail. I wanted to expose whatever was necessary to keep her comfortable.

Before my grandfather died, he gave me the secret to a successful relationship. It was very simple advice. *G, communicate to a woman verbally and nonverbally that she is your queen and everything else will fall into place*, he said in his favorite rocking chair. I learned that lesson a little too late when I destroyed the opportunity to hold on to my college sweetheart.

Trying to maintain my status of Mr. Popular, I fell victim to all the attention the girls gave me. In the process, I hurt a princess who was admired by half the male population at Stockhem University. Vanya Sanders had the most beautiful dark complexion I had ever seen. She was one third Seminole, Cuban, and African American. Somewhere in that mixture was a white relative. I called her Black Butter because her skin looked creamy and always felt soft.

Vanya and I were finishing the first semester of our senior year when we were getting ready to head out to Stockhem's holiday ball. The fall semester was coming to a close. Our relationship was sweet, but I made it sour while seeking the attention of any girl who would take my bait. I was smooth and so was my rap. I chose to be with Vanya because she liked me, not because I wore my fraternity letters or had all access passes to the athletic games. I helped to manage the football and basketball teams at Stockhem. That made me attractive to a number of women on campus. Vanya, she was truth. She loved me for reasons no one else could understand.

I was nervous about our arrival at the ball because one of the neophytes of Beta Theta Mu took me seriously when I told her to save a dance for me. She replied, *I'll be in the black slip dress without panties.* Beta girl's comment continued to replay in my head the moment I set foot into the ballroom. She knew I was seeing Vanya. However, Vanya knew nothing about her. Beta girl made it clear that she was interested in only one thing and what Vanya didn't know she wouldn't tell. I had to be careful.

An hour passed. I thought I was safe until I noticed Beta Girl near the buffet table. She was eating chocolate covered strawberries as she watched me dance with Vanya. She winked at me and held up the numbers five two and three. I assumed that was her suite number. Beta Girl pointed to her watch and held up ten fingers. She walked away and my eyes lowered to her backside. She really wasn't wearing any underwear.

As fate would have it, Vanya's cousin came over to take pictures. The two of them began to engage in the usual act of compliments on their attire. Vanya looked wonderful in her red dress. Somehow, that wasn't good enough for me at that moment. I excused myself and allowed the cousins to continue their girly chatter. Ten minutes passed and I went to meet the hands of time that began to change the course of my relationship with Vanya and ultimately the way I governed myself with women.

When I reached room 523, Beta Girl lay naked and crossways on the king-sized bed. She was surrounded by rose petals. Candles were lit in each corner of the room. Luther was singing, *If Only For One Night*. She had the moment planned out. The playboy in me couldn't let the moment pass. I took advantage of the situation, thinking only of myself. I made sure I used protection because if she was setting it out for me, no telling who else had a piece of her action. Although she was satisfaction guaranteed, I understood, moments after committing the act of indiscretion against Vanya, the true meaning of, *a few moments of pleasure can give you a lifetime of pain*.

After a quick wash in the bathroom, I looked at the time. I needed to get back to the ballroom before Vanya noticed I was missing. Beta Girl walked me to the door. She leaned in for a kiss before closing it behind me. She told me to call if I wanted another ride. God had a funny way of whooping my tail because just as I backed away from Beta Girl's lips, Vanya and her cousin turned the corner leading to the hallway where I was standing. I was caught and had little room for vindication.

I tried to salvage the relationship after letting Vanya filter her emotions for two weeks. No roses, teddy bear, nor singing telegrams were good enough to make up for the pain I caused. She made that clear with her consistent silent treatment.

After winter break, Vanya finally returned my calls and made plans to come by my apartment just off Stockhem's campus. She let me hug her and I didn't want to let go. I assured her that I was no longer seeing Beta Girl and that she transferred to another school. I thought that would make things easier for us so that we could move forward in our relationship. Yet, nothing could prepare me for what was to come next.

Vanya began to explain to me why she was in the guest suites area of the country club. She had reserved a suite for us because she wanted to tell me in the right atmosphere that she was carrying my seed. She wanted to surprise me.

I didn't know how to respond to the news. My eyes started to fill with tears. I loved Vanya, but I had been too selfish to say no to a stallion with a backside that could win a war. My mind raced with preparatory plans for us and the baby. I was ready to marry Vanya even before graduation. We didn't have to worry about money because I had accepted a job as a copy editor for a paper in Atlanta. In the midst of all my excitement, Vanya stopped me. She ushered me to a seat. I was too anxious to sit and continued flapping my lips. Before I knew it, she burst into tears and buried her head in my chest. She was going to have an abortion. She had made the appointment for the next day and just wanted to give me the courtesy of knowing that I had fathered a child.

Every function of my soul froze and then shattered like glass from the hit. Her words shot me. I was torn. I internally shed the blood of a baby who wasn't going to have a chance to come into the world. I suffered the pain for my son or my daughter who would never be.

I spent the next three hours trying to convince Vanya not to terminate the pregnancy. She insisted that it was the right thing to do declaring that if she couldn't trust me to be faithful to her there was no way she could trust that I would be a loyal father. I told her to trust God. She looked at me with violent eyes.

"Don't talk about God after what you did!" shot from her mouth.

I looked beyond the surface of her eyes and saw emptiness. Her love for me had hollowed. She left my apartment at the same time she left my life. I never saw Vanya after graduation. She never even said goodbye.

Two days after Vanya's last visit, I made my way to church. That was something I had not done while enrolled at Stockhem. *Train a child in the way they should go and they shall not depart from it.* Thank God for my mother's weekly coercion of sending me to Sunday school and joining the junior usher board. God was the only answer to break me out of my depression of losing my first love and my first child because of my stupidity. I knew if I was hurting, Vanya's pain had to be twice as bad. I accepted Christ with full understanding that Sunday and developed my five cardinal rules of dating.

1. Appreciate the gifts God gives me.

2. Follow my grandfather's advice to treat the woman in my life as a queen.

3. Think with my brain and heart.

4. Don't lay with anyone that I wouldn't take as my wife.

5. Never put myself in any position where a woman would want to abort my child because I gave her reason to question my integrity.

Although it took me eight years to find her, I was confident that I could be true to Dolly—if she would have me. While I was telling her the story of Vanya, she listened attentively with invisible antennas taking in all I said. I didn't want to hide my past or portray a false representation of myself. When I finished speaking, she stared in silence before responding.

"Well, that was quite a story."

"It's what was, Dolly. I'm not a Buddhist, but karma came back to haunt me."

"I don't understand."

"I tried love again some years later and my girlfriend stepped-out on me. I thought that was my payback, so I stayed in the relationship. However, cheating became more frequent and I then had the courage to just let it go. My life wasn't worth it."

"Hmmph!" she exclaimed. "Doesn't feel so good on the other end, does it?"

"Not at all," I agreed. I moved in closer to her and grabbed both her hands and said to her, "Look, I'm not perfect, but I will do what's necessary to keep you interested. You could be my best friend."

"And how do you know this?"

"Look at us. We're on the couch, curled up talkin' after watching the game. Straight chillin'. You're a man's dream."

Dolly wasn't just some piece of ass for an evening. I felt the need to be candid with her about my past. I wanted to know all of her and for her to understand the man I could be in her life. I didn't want to push her. I kissed her on the cheek and told her I'd give her some time to consider me as her suitor.

She said, "Thank you, I'll pray on it."

It was getting late. I concluded the evening with a hug and told her to check her email in the morning.

To dhunter@dcrealty.com
From gerald.washington@blockwriters.com
Date September 13, 2004
Subject Lunch, Movie, Dinner

Doll,

I hope you're still smiling after last night. I had a great time. Let's do lunch on Wednesday...dinner and a movie on Thursday...and let Friday make plans for us before my set at the club. The world is yours.

-Gerald

CHAPTER ELEVEN
Spa Ladies

My girls
My friends
My sistahs
'Til the end
One bride-to-be
Two single hearts linger
Three bonded by love

My girls
My friends
My sistahs
'Til the end
Taking a break on a Friday
PEACE.

Erica was getting married in less than a month. She was scheduled to travel to South Carolina to participate in pre-wedding activities with relatives and friends who would be unable to attend the ceremony. Before her departure, she wanted to reserve time exclusively with Cita and me at a spa . I shouldn't have expected anything less from my country, Ivy League friend.

After finishing Hampton, Erica enrolled into the University of Pennsylvania's MBA program. She had no problem admitting, upon graduation, that she promised to enjoy the finer things in life. Even with that said, listening to her you'd think she was still a Charleston girl. You could take the girl out of South Carolina but South Carolina was stained in the girl. Regardless of where Erica was reared or educated, Richard Bailey accepted her. They met during our first homecoming in undergrad and she never let him out of her site from that moment on. Their happily ever after was soon to come.

Richard attended all the HUs of prestige. He received his B.S. from Hampton University, his M.A. from Howard University, and received his J.D. from Harvard University's School of Law. Richard was fine and educated. Erica hit the jackpot. As well versed as he is, you would think he had a shee shee foo attitude. On the contrary, Richard was one of the most down to earth bruthas I've had the pleasure of knowing. He had to be to marry Erica. She's a full-time job.

Cita and I reserved a luxury car for our girls day out with Erica. We indulged in a continental breakfast with mimosas for them and a regular orange juice for me. Instead of frequenting Blackplatinum Café as we would on any given Friday, we took the day off to pamper the bride-to-be. We planned to eat pizza and ice cream and curl up in front of Cita's big screen to watch chick flicks for the last time before Erica said, *I do.* I had to postpone my Friday rendezvous with Gerald because I wasn't about to get in trouble with Ms. Erica. He was sad but understood.

We arrived at the day spa by eight that morning. We got the works: seaweed body wraps, hot stone massages, manicures and pedicures with a paraffin wax, and hair and make-up sessions. I was surprised that Cita allowed another stylist to touch our hair or hers for that matter. She's been doing our hair since 1995, the year she moved from New Orleans and became my next door neighbor on South Dakota Avenue.

Cita hooked us up in the basement of her mother's house when all she had was a jar of perm, a hair dryer, a flat iron, and some rollers. While at Hampton, Erica and I waited for the holiday breaks in college to get our touch-ups done by Cita. Our campus coif had been a tightly pulled ponytail with gel and water until Cita could lay her magic touch on it.

Thanks to an inheritance her father left, Cita was able to open her own shop on Pennsylvania Avenue. She didn't talk much about the amount, so Erica and I didn't pry. We were just glad we could count on Cita to keep us looking good.

The jazz music in the day spa reminded me of the first night I saw Gerald on stage. *A Night in Tunisia* made me recollect one evening we sat in his car at Haines Point. At the risk of seeming fresh, Gerald reached over to my side of the 750 Li and pressed a button that made the seat hug me.

"This is how tight I want to hold you, Dolly," he admitted while looking in my eyes. "I'm not going to let you get away." At that moment, he opened the sunroof and like magic, three shooting stars danced across the sky. He held my hand and we both made three wishes.

I continued to zone out as Erica griped about some of the vendors she used for the wedding. Ms. Erica wanted everything to be perfect and wished she could take back the moment she told her cousin, Lawanda, she could coordinate the wedding plans. Erica eventually took over and just let her cousin think she did something worthwhile. In my relaxed state, I tuned her out and dozed off. Although brief, my nap captured a moment yet to be played out between Gerald and I:

We were in the Caribbean walking along the shore in white linen. My hair was in twists with a purple tulip adorning the right side of my head. Gerald's upper body was exposed as he had his shirt unbuttoned. It was blowing in the wind in slow motion. My smile was a mile wide as we swung our hands and gazed into each other's eyes. We played in the water and built sand castles on the beach. Chasing the seagulls, I tripped and Gerald quickly came to my rescue. He placed one hand on the back of my head and caressed my face with the other to make sure I was okay. It was like something out of a sitcom on Valentine's Day with guitars playing and Michael McDonald on vocals. Nevertheless, it was an enjoyable site to dream that was stopped in midstream when I heard the giggles of my two best friends.

"That's some dream you're having there gal."

"Yeah, here I am thinkin' this time was 'bout me and yo head is in the clouds with that man," Erica joked.

"What are you two talkin' about?"

Mimicking, Cita said, "Oh Gerald, stop! You'll get sand in my hair."

"I didn't say that."

"You sho did! Look here, gal, jess get ya rump up. Your

masseuse was finished witcha 'bout ten minutes ago. I tipped him to let ya sleep off that dream 'cause we have enough to blackmail yo tail with in three weeks."

"Three weeks? What's happening in three weeks besides your wedding, Erica?"

"Oh! Erica didn't tell you that she invited Gerald to the wedding?"

I gave Erica a bewildered look. "That's right. He'll sho nuff be there. 'Cause I knew you weren't goin' to invite him. So, don't trip down the aisle."

Every time I tried to question her motives or make a comment about her betrayal, she silenced me with a, *Shh*. Gerald's attendance changed everything about my promenade down the aisle with my selected groomsman. I was already self-conscious about Erica's wedding guests watching me. Including Gerald in the equation made my position as a maid-of-honor more unbearable. I was going to be like the S.S. Minnow, a shipwreck, but in a giddy sort of way.

I had three weeks to get myself together. My preparation included increased exercise to decrease my thunder thighs. Although firm, they were still hefty. My usual lunch out with Gerald had to be reduced from entrees to sandwiches and soups. Cita was going to need to make sure my hair-do was as flawless as the bride's come the wedding day. I had to be tight from head to toe. When it was time for us to go to the pedicure station, I asked the operator to perform an extra special scrub on my feet. I made future pedicure appointments each week leading up to the wedding. Flour kickers would not be a good sight to see.

Our spa day proved to be beneficial. Erica was glowing. Cita had the day off from serving clients at her salon. I enjoyed being pampered. When our bottoms hit the seats of the

Lincoln our eyes closed in slumber. My dream of Gerald and I on the beach continued. This time, it wasn't interrupted. It concluded with a kiss as the sun descended from the sky. Can dreams come true? A little hope made me believe they would. In the meantime, I just had to wait to see how the story would unfold.

CHAPTER TWELVE
Old Fish, New Fish

Ever notice other fish swimming in your pond
Flapping their fins
Blowing big bubbles
To impress beautiful sea creatures?
In cool waters
You don't sweat.
With straight-faced confidence
And a net,
Catch the beautiful one.
Burst the bubbles
And swim away with the prize.

I stopped by Blackplatinum on a Friday morning to speak with the house manager. I wanted to put my boy, Chico, on the Saturday night slate. He was moving to Northern Virginia from Tampa and needed something to do in his spare time. He played the bass guitar, a great compliment to an already awesome band. The manager agreed to put him on the stage. If the crowd liked him, he could stay. If not, he had to go. That was a good compromise. I was sure the Café audience would welcome him with open arms. On my way out Jimmy stopped me.

"Telegram for Blacksax." I was baffled. I wasn't expecting any news.

"I'm gonna start charging you for all these love notes, man."

"Love notes?" I grabbed the envelope and found an invitation and a message. It seemed that one of Dolly's friends was getting married in a couple of weeks and wanted me to attend. My only instructions: look nice and show up. It was signed *Erica, Dolly's friend.* I've always known the women in D.C. to be aggressive, but I didn't know how deep the aggression ran.

It didn't seem like a Dolly gesture to send someone else to do her, pardon the expression, dirty work. Nonetheless, I thanked Jimmy, checked my calendar and saw that I was available. I was assured that Dolly would be happy to see me based on our recurrent afternoons and evenings together. Her response to my daily emails to take her out to lunch or to catch a movie in the evening was enough to make me feel secure. She may have rejected a date once or twice and that's only because they conflicted with her work schedule. Even then, we found ways to make up for missed time. We would bowl a few games later that evening or take a trip to Dave and Buster's right after work.

Dating Dolly became more and more routine. We began to see each other almost every day. In fact, being with her was like a large dose of oxygen. She helped me breathe through the rest of my day at *Block Writers*. Without Dolly's energy, I am drained like Superman in the presence of Kryptonite.

After leaving the club, I parked my car at the subway station and headed for the recreation center on Benning Road in northeast D.C.. I play basketball once a week with a few of the neighborhood boys. They would meet me and another volunteer on Fridays after school. We usually treated them to a meal at McDonald's to have a rap session.

"Come on, Washington, D-up! I know you're not scared of a fifteen-year-old."

"Sucka, please! I was stealin' balls 'fore yo mama was even born."

"Pass the ball, T-Rock!"

"Nigga, I got this!"

"Watch your mouth, Terrence."

"My bad, Washington."

I took the ball in the midst of his distraction.

"Game point!"

"That's what's up! The youngins get to treat us today, fellaz!" Sam, one of the other volunteers shouted from center court.

"See man, I told you to pass the ball."

"Shut up, Mark."

"That's enough guys. Just go pack up so we can head to Black Mac." We called the McDonald's Black Mac because the neighborhood was predominately black and that was the establishment's number one patronage.

The old heads had a victory for the first time in three weeks. My motivation: I pictured Dolly on the sideline in a red and white cheerleading uniform waving pom-poms to the same rhythm of her bouncing ponytails. The thought kept me smiling. It made me show off my skills on the court.

"Yo, Washington, you were on your game today, son. First win in three weeks, right?" Sam remarked while stuffing his gym bag.

"Well, if you got it, what else is there to say?"

"Sam, I'll tell you who has him on his A-game," a voice from the gymnasium door shouted. It was Jupiter.

"Come on, Jupe, man!" He walked toward the bleachers where Sam and I stood.

He had apparently overheard our conversation in the hallway. He was coming into the rec center to give free drum lessons to registered members in the community. The room he used was next to the gym.

"Do tell, brother Jupiter."

"My niece, Dolly."

"Hold up! You were supposed to hook me up with her two years ago."

"Yeah, well, I lied. Sam, you don't have your shit together, man!"

"That's messed up, Jupe."

"Well, it is the truth, man. You're still at home with yo mama," I cosigned and Sam threw a towel at me.

"I heard ya'll yappin' in here and stopped in to say hello. Now pass me that ball to see if I still got game."

I honored his wish. He bounced the ball a couple of times, wiped his brow, then shot the ball. Swoosh! Three-points right in the trash can beside the locker room. Sam and I tried to hide our laughter by pulling the top of our shirts over our mouths.

We tossed our bags over our shoulders and hit Jupiter on the back. Just when we reached the side exit, Jupiter shouted, "Oh yeah, you boys come by my house tomorrow. I'm having a seafood cookout at three."

A seafood cookout? I had the gas face on but managed to sound like I knew what he was talking about and replied, "Alright man, I'll call you for the details." Turns out, Jupiter sponsors an annual gathering of family and friends at his house to say goodbye to summer and hello to fall. He fires up the grill on one of the last warm days in October and the attendees bring seafood for the potluck. He had enough backyard space for at least one hundred fifty people. Since I was a rookie to the event, I was responsible for one bushel of crabs. Besides the roadside trucks along Central Avenue in Capitol Heights, Maryland, I knew of only one place to get crabs in D.C.: the wharf.

After eating my super-sized number one, I headed to Rhode Island Avenue Station to get my whip. I wanted to see what a bushel of crabs would run me. I made a left off Rhode Island to get on 7th Street. Rush hour traffic was almost non-existent on this Friday evening. I zoomed through the streets. I was glad the cops weren't out.

It was approaching six o'clock. The Smithsonian tourists were still walking along The Mall with their disposable cameras. Many were anxious to get a shot of the Capitol just as the day was coming to an end. Souvenir bags were hanging on baby strollers while mothers read maps and fathers were less than enthused about the next destination. The museums were closed so that should have provided some source of comfort for them. They were closer to reaching their goal of catching the Friday evening highlights on ESPN. I managed to smile despite the frowns of my fellow male tourists.

When I saw the Capitol on my left I grinned while reflecting on the first time Dolly and I spent the afternoon just a few blocks from the traffic light on Independence and 7th Streets. She was my Hope Diamond and I hoped she would be the jewel in my life.

I finally reached the wharf after having to pass the many government agencies along my tour de downtown D.C.. I had to search for a space to park my ride. Nearby club goers beat me to the good spaces. Club H20 was the happening place on any given weekend. I prayed there would be a spot somewhere near the seafood vendors. I took my chances circling the waterfront. To my surprise, I saw Dolly conversing with a man. Her neck-twisting and finger-pointing lead me to believe this wasn't a pleasant dialogue. There was an urgency to make my acquaintance known.

My prayers were answered. A car pulled out of the circle just outside the market area. I grabbed it. I had to rescue my jewel from the hands of a thief. I had to be crafty in my approach. The last thing I wanted to do was scare her and get into a competition with this cat. I refused to allow her to be the one to get away because I was crass. I had to be proactive while reeling in my catch of the day. She wasn't getting caught on someone else's hook if I had anything to do with it.

CHAPTER THIRTEEN
Wilted Flowers

Seeds fertilized
Leaves growing
Sprouting from the ground
Buds blooming

Blowing winds
Rain transforming into tears
Dew Drops
Tears Drop
Petals Drop

Blowing winds
Trampled by treacherous hands
Darkness without light
Even with little hope
Wilted flowers still grow.

U ncle James and Aunt Nell invited family and friends over for their annual barbecue and seafood feast. It was usually held on a Sunday after church but this year it fell on a Saturday afternoon. The weatherman predicted rain on the scheduled day. Local pastors even came by with their Tupperware plates and coolers full of ribs to Unc's house in Bowie. I was responsible for the shrimp and crab salad. I took a trip to the wharf for fresh ingredients.

Summer had waved goodbye to its chirping birds and fully blossomed flowers. So I thought I would get a good deal on my seafood purchase.

"Sir, these are medium shrimp in the fall. Why are you charging me beginning of the summer prices?"

"Look lady, the sign says twelve dollars a pound."

"I'll give you twenty-five dollars for three pounds and I'll cook 'em myself."

"Read the sign, Miss."

"The lady said she'll give you twenty-five dollars, in cash, for three pounds."

I hesitated before turning around. The voice was so distinct it scared me.

"Mickey Hunter."

There was only one person who called me Mickey. There was only one person who could say it and make my heart melt. It was the same person who turned on my tears and never came back to turn them off. Jersey Phillips, the last man I had ever loved. He was the man who ran away with my heart in his back pocket. He was the reason I had turned into the spider woman.

I said a silent prayer for strength before I faced my nemesis. "Hello, Jersey." He took twenty-five dollars out of his inside jacket pocket, winked at the fisherman, and turned his attention back to me.

"You look good, Mickey."

"I know," I said while rolling my eyes. "and my name is Darlene."

"Oh," he chuckled. "I'm sorry, Darlene."

I looked through my wallet so I could pay him back. Then I thought about it. It was the least he could do for his abrupt departure at the altar some four years prior.

"Thanks for the shrimp."

"You're welcome."

He ran his hand across my face. It was fixed in a scowling position.

"Ma'am?"

The fisherman called and handed me the bag of shrimp.

I proceeded to walk off and Jersey tried to pull me back.

"Jersey, I really don't have much to say to you."

I paused, looked in the air and began again. I went into sistah-girl mode: shaking my finger in his face while the head moved to the rhythm of my twisting neck.

"On second thought, you are an absolute disappointment to good men." I commenced to move closer and he reached out to embrace me.

"Mickey, I'm so sorry for the way I left things."

Just on the edge of my peripheral was a black Beemer. I zoomed in to find that it was Gerald. He saw me too and slowed down to slide into a parking space.

"Look, Jersey, you should have just told me you didn't want to marry me instead of wasting my family's time and money. Were we not worth the truth? And your secret lovers?

That took the cake. You jeopardized my life and embarrassed the hell out of me in front of everyone who mattered to me in this world." I had years of frustration built up and I was ready to release it all on him. Fortunately for him, he was saved by my hot rod.

"What's the problem here?" Gerald was stern in his approach.

"Who are you?" JP asked powerfully as if I was still his woman.

I wrapped my arms around Gerald and replied, "Oh! Are you wondering who this real man is coming to be beside his queen?" I hugged Gerald closer to me.

"Mickey, at that time my ex-wife was so upset about me remarrying and the baby——-"

"Ex-wife? The baby? Don't let me start on babies," I exploded with fury and started to charge toward him. Gerald grabbed me just before my open palm met the side of Jersey's face. As handsome as JP was, he was the ugliest man alive when our paths crossed that day.

"You know what, Doll, let's just get outta here." Gerald eyed Jersey in disgust and then proceeded to escort me to my car. We walked away leaving Jersey standing with the fisherman and the rest of the sea creatures on ice.

"Mickey, I never stopped loving you!" Jersey shouted.

I waved my hand in the *whatever* motion and kept walking without looking back.

"You can be a fire cracker when you want to be. Are you okay?"

"Yeah."

"Wanna talk about it?"

Of course I wanted to talk about it. However, doing so would expose a part of me I was scared for Gerald to see, a dark and vulnerable side. I wasn't sure of the depth of our friendship. So, I stalled until I realized he had a genuine interest in the details.

"Darlene?"

"Gerald, I don't know if you really want to hear the story."

"Look, if we're going to build a strong friendship, I need you to be as open and honest with me as possible. Whatever it is, I am here to help you, not hurt you."

I sighed. He waited with patient eyes. I looked away.

"Darlene, talk to me. Whatever it is or was we can get through it together."

Wow. Together. It's an eight letter, three syllable word that meant so much when dealing with the matters of the heart. "Okay, Gerald," I began to tell him the story.

Jersey and I started dating during my last year of Hampton's 5 year teaching program. The fifth year afforded me the opportunity to receive my MA. I was working as a student teacher in the Hampton Roads area. He was an administrator from the charter school board in D.C.. I was pre-occupied with keeping my students in line when Jersey walked passed my classroom. Jersey was touring the building with other guests. I felt bodies move by my doorway. I quickly glanced in the direction of the visitors and waved hello. I didn't want to interrupt the learning environment with verbal greetings. I continued with my lesson. As I was moving about the student workstations, I noticed there was still someone in my doorway.

He was very tall in stature with salt and pepper hair. I could tell by his smile upon the subtle licking of his lips that he was checking me out. I was flattered, but I couldn't take my attention off my students. During my lunch break, I checked my mailbox in the teacher's lounge. Under my *Educational Leadership* magazine I found a handwritten envelope with my name on it. It was a note from Jersey *JP* Phillips. An invitation to dinner was extended. He identified himself as the man who couldn't break away from my doorway. I gladly accepted with my gullible self. I loved the attention. I felt desired.

The dinner was nice and more dinners followed. He traveled back and forth to Hampton at least twice a month. The weekends he wasn't visiting me, he sent airline tickets for me to meet him at some conference he had to attend.

After I finished Hampton, I moved back to D.C. and JP got me a job at a charter school. Jersey and I began to spend more intimate moments together. Weekend trips to the mountains, formal galas, and several evenings in each other's arms made up the foundation of our relationship.

Jersey was a perfect gentleman and quite the romantic. His only vice, loving me while separated from his second wife. After our third year together, he did finalize the divorce and soon thereafter proposed to me. Jersey's third attempt at marriage should have been the biggest red flag on the planet. I couldn't see it because at the time I didn't care. I had grown to love him and everything about him. I just assumed those women weren't capable of meeting the responsibilities of being his wife. I was going to be the exception. In fact, he told me they weren't able to be the wives he needed in the kitchen, bedroom, or for the children he wanted to reproduce.

Gerald was shocked to even hear that I would take anything less than first string. At the point where he met me, Gerald was right. Aunt Nell said I was as naïve as a doorknob leading to hell. I admitted to Gerald that I hadn't loved myself enough to accept only the best. I had been too busy making other people happy and seeing that their needs were met. There was almost nothing I wouldn't do for friends and family that I loved. Although my ducks seemed to be in a row, dealing with the forth-coming pain was a time in my past that I never wanted to revisit. I dealt with disappointments in relationships before, but this one was the mother of all breakups.

I had accepted the proposal and Jersey gave me six months to plan. He wanted to marry me right away. He didn't want to go another year without me being Mrs. Darlene *Mickey* Phillips. The ring was gorgeous. I felt guilty wearing a paperweight, but it was mine.

My girls didn't care for him. They tolerated him out of respect for me. Cita took the careful approach by not giving me suggestions but just referred to scripture regarding divorce. She voiced her concern days before the wedding. She left a post-it on my refrigerator door citing a verse from *Malachi 2:16: I hate divorce, says the Lord God of Israel* and *Matthew 19:9: I tell you that anyone who divorces his wife, except for marital unfaithfulness, and marries another woman commits adultery.*

After reading the scriptures, I had some thinking to do. Even in my meditation and revisiting why Jersey divorced both his wives, I was still going on with the wedding. The next morning, I was dressed in my white gown ready to enter into a covenant with a pure heart and with pure love for Jersey. Nothing mattered because I was certain that I would spend the rest of my life with him. I was the one he waited to rightfully take his last name.

I was as nervous as any first bride. Yet, I was ready. Cita and Erica were on stand-by with Kleenex, hair pins, and a spare pair of panty hose. We didn't know that the Kleenex would really come in handy.

Uncle James and my dad were giving me away. They were in the bridal suite waiting with me while marveling at how beautiful I looked. Twenty minutes prior to the processional, my mother stormed through the door in tears. She handed me a letter that was left on the altar. It was from Jersey. Apparently, he had an emergency call from his second ex-wife. She was having their child and that's why he couldn't go on with the nuptials. He needed to be a father to his first born. The kicker was that after all this happened, I missed my cycle and found out I was having his baby too. If that wasn't enough, I was later informed that JP had also been in a relationship with two other women and one of his lovers threatened to expose him at the ceremony.

When I confronted him about the information from my anonymous source, JP said that he couldn't jeopardize his position with the school board and had the nerve to ask me not to disclose the details to the public. He was more concerned about his image than anyone else who may have been hurt in the process. Turns out, his claim to fame was preying on young girls on their way out of college. I couldn't get to the doctor's office fast enough to get tested for HIV. Thank God, my results came back negative.

Just after entering my second trimester, I had a miscarriage due to the excessive stress and lack of nourishment. Losing the baby killed me softly. I had started becoming attached and although no one told me, I knew a little girl was growing inside me. From this experience, I entered a very dark place in my life where extreme depression took hold. I became lifeless and only moved through life mechanically. I was no longer a functioning member of society. Cita and Erica came over often, but felt I needed 24 hour surveillance. Since my parents were in New York, Uncle James and Aunt Nell were the closest relatives to me. They suggested that I move into their house until I got myself together.

I lived off the personal savings I had tucked away in the bank for rainy days. I was living through a thunderstorm so my circumstances qualified for use of the funds. I stayed in my room and left only to eat a bowl of cereal for breakfast, to shower for work, and to dine off my nightly vegetable soup and cranberry juice for dinner. I was in such an abyss that my work as a teacher suffered. My attendance was poor.

It took me six months to get out of the funk. In that time, I turned my life over to Jesus and turned into a love hermit. I reserved my heart only for Him until it was time to share it with another. I wasn't willing to risk the possibility of another broken heart. I wanted to rely on the Lord for emotional dependence and comfort. It seemed the only safe love to hold.

When the school year ended, I wasn't asked to return to teach another year. As summer approached, I decided to take some real estate classes and successfully passed my exams. It was then that I found a renewed spirit and selling homes became the new love of my life. It had taken me two years to even consider a man's offer to take me out. I dated but with a distant heart and watchful eyes. Gerald was the first person I seriously considered since the JP incident.

Gerald was a good listener. I was choked up on my tears but he never interrupted me and waited until I collected myself before making any remarks. I expected an array of questions but he simply stretched out his arms and allowed me to find comfort in hearing his heartbeat. I could hear the sweet sound of his blood rushing through his veins and exhaled.

"*Know that the Lord is God. We are his people, and the sheep of his pasture.*" I listened as he quoted scripture. I lifted my head from his embrace.

"Dolly, you're a flower and you're growing. I'll pray with you during your days of drought."

I was speechless. I could only stare into his eyes while my adrenaline raced from the bottom of my feet to the top of my head. I was then very glad that Erica had invited him to the wedding. I hoped, at that moment, that he would watch my garden grow. Gerald liberated me from love's vice, disappointment.

I was so caught up in discussing my life episode involving JP that I forgot to ask him why he was at the wharf in the first place. It turns out Uncle James invited him to the barbecue seafood feast. He was pricing a bushel of crabs. I neglected to invite him because we were trying to keep the details of our relationship private until we knew exactly where things would go. Although optimistic, I didn't want to make the public announcement in case things didn't turn out the way we expected. I wanted to prevent a retraction from being printed in the *Dolly Daily Tribune*, i.e. I didn't want to explain more than was necessary.

The long lapse between receiving and returning Cita and Erica's calls may have caused them to think I was spending more time with Gerald. The increased attention from Gerald at Blackplatinum was also a clue that we were closer than either of us let on.

Gerald asked me to wait in my car while he got a quote for the crabs. He placed an order of two bushels for the next day. He made a request to have the crabs steamed and doused with Old Bay seasoning. I was in awe because few people north of Maryland and south of Northern Virginia know about the good Old Bay.

My escort followed me home to make sure I was safe. Before entering my development, we picked up some Popeye's. Gerald stayed with me for an hour before heading to Blackplatinum. He gave me instructions to take a warm bath and relax before heading to the club. I told him not to be alarmed if I wasn't there on time. The bath was probably going to take longer than expected. Calgon was going to take me away and I was going to drift with the current. My JP blues had to be washed away.

CHAPTER THIRTEEN
Wedding Melodies

Here comes the bride
Floating down the aisle
Like a feather fallen from an angel's wings.

The onlookers' eyes
Fill with tears
While lips smile.

The groom waits anxiously
At the altar.
His heart races.
His adrenaline rises.
As she reaches her knight in shining armor,
Papa holds a little tighter
As this will be the last time he can call her his baby girl
But proud to share her with the man who will love her like
a princess.
It's time to give her away.
Gazing into each other's eyes,
Their souls meet before God's throne.
The vow of a lifetime is made.
An exchange of never ending circles
Each finger is wrapped like a present.
In a covenant unbroken,
They say, "I do."

YOLONDA D. COLEMAN

The groom salutes his bride
And before the first kiss as man and wife
He catches the single tear of joy from her eye and says,
"I will love you for life."

D olly and I grew closer with each vulnerable moment we shared from our past. Spiritually, we were developing. When *Block Writers* was seemingly falling low on subscriptions or other sales promotions weren't quite up to par, Dolly and I would pray together. When a client was ready to close on a property and decided days before settlement to withdraw, I'd let her sulk on my shoulder while I read a Psalm to her. It was her favorite book in the Bible.

We alternated days to provide a scripture through email. It was our daily devotion. When we met for lunch, we would discuss the Word and make it a point to apply it to our lives. If we made a breakthrough personally or professionally, we'd instantly share by leaving voicemails or emails. I will admit that the success of the magazine increased when my daily prayer life with Dolly increased.

Even though the Bible became our favorite book to read, our schedules didn't permit us to worship together on Sundays. I was either scheduled to play in the church band for the morning and afternoon services or she was scheduled to teach Sunday school. We just accepted that God would eventually make a way for us to enter His house together in His time, not ours.

On my way to Erica's wedding, I faced Woodrow Wilson traffic. There was an accident just after Indian Head Highway. Instead of getting frustrated I just meditated on my recent memories.

Arriving at Jupiter's crib in Bowie was less than well choreographed. I looked drunk stumbling into his backyard with two bushels of crabs. I smelled of Old Bay and the Potomac

River. I tried to spray some cologne to offset the smell to no avail. It was a good thing Dolly hadn't arrived yet. I just prayed the breeze would get the scent out of my clothes.

I found Jupiter grilling next to the lanai. A few of the band members and Jimmy were drinking and cuttin' up with him. I met Fingaz for the first time. He left the wife and new born back at home. It was the first time he had been out since the baby was born. Other guests filled the basement and the rest of his three-level home. Jupiter encouraged everyone to go out in the backyard, but few made their way to the green. I was introduced to Jupiter's wife who was stretched out in a recliner near the floor model television. I was tagged as his adopted nephew when meeting Jupiter's family and friends. He winked at me as if he held on to a secret I was yet to discover. Doll's parents weren't in attendance. They were still in Aruba celebrating the anniversary of the day they met. I was hoping to meet the people responsible for producing Dolly.

Most of the family that came through Jupiter's spot were his in-laws. It was at his barbecue that I found out he was a Moss and not a Hunter. He and Dolly's mother were siblings. The Hunter side of the family, apparently, was all together different. The Hunters were so spread out across the country that they only got together once a year. Thanksgiving doubled as their reunion.

The family meets in North Carolina the Wednesday night before Thanksgiving until the Sunday after. The Hunters shut down the city of Weldon. Richmond International was the closest major airport and it's 75 miles away. The staff prepared for the heavy traffic of the family that travels from as far west as Seattle and as far north as Rhode Island. Greyhound and Amtrak attendants knew most of the family by name.

There are some 250 Hunters that invade Halifax County every year. Sunday service at Faith United Missionary Baptist

Church of God in Christ is closed to the general public from 9am to 11am when the Hunters are in town. The community center is reserved a year in advance for the annual brunch after service. Dolly was a little more than modest when she told me about the size of her family. If Jupiter hadn't introduced me to Dolly's Uncle Lyle Hunter, Jupiter's best friend, I would have been in the dark about Doll's family tree. It was cool though.

Dolly arrived just after four o'clock. She and her friends trotted into the party with bowls and bags. I made an attempt to assist the ladies. In doing so, I clumsily tripped over a bag of charcoal near the grill. My game was slipping.

"Look out, baby," an elderly lady shouted from a lawn chair.

Dolly saw me and shook her head with a grin. I didn't fall, but the fumble alone made me want to jet. She walked up beside me.

"Enjoy your trip, honey?" She kissed me on the cheek.

"Aaaah! The lady has jokes."

"Hey, Sax," Cita shouted in my direction. I grabbed her Safeway bag. I smelled red beans, rice, and sausage. Dolly mentioned that Cita was part Creole. I couldn't wait to dig into her dish. I did a double take while reaching to help Erica and Dolly with their things. Cita's uncommonly thick hair reminded me of Vanya's long locks. Cita wore it in a long French braid that crawled down her back. It seemed an appropriate hairstyle for the occasion, out of the way.

"I hope you're coming to my wedding." Erica's comment broke me out of my reminiscent thoughts. I gave her a nod to assure her I'd be there and then reached to help her with the bags.

"Oh, I have it. Thanks anyway."

Dolly walked over to the picnic table, placed a bowl in the

center, and removed the foil. I expected her seafood salad to be off the chain because she never did show up to Blackplatinum the previous evening. The bath I instructed her to take must have been a welcomed treat. I would have enjoyed being a fly on the wall to watch Dolly in a relaxed state covered in bubbles.

"Did you put your foot in this dish, baby?"

"Here," she grabbed a plate and serving spoon, "let me help you find out."

She scooped two big spoonfuls of the seafood salad on a plate and surprisingly fed me a taste. It was better than I anticipated. Lump crab meat, tuna, shrimp, and lobster pieces were mixed in with macaroni, relish, onions, and a tangy spice I couldn't put my finger on. She used Miracle Whip instead of mayonnaise. I know this because I only use the salad spread on my sandwiches. If I knew Dolly could burn in the kitchen, I would have saved a lot of money on taking her out to eat. I'd choose a home cooked meal over mass produced food any day.

Beep! Beep! Beep! My thoughts were interrupted. The driver behind me blew his horn frantically. Traffic was moving and I was sitting still. I looked at the digital clock on my dashboard. I still had plenty of time to make it to the wedding. I pulled down the sun visor to get the directions to the Floral Hills Country Club. I had to take the exit for Route 1 in Alexandria. The wedding ceremony was about five miles off the beltway exit. I followed the brown signs to the site.

Upon approaching the club, I saw a guard's station booth. Once I was confirmed as a guest for the Lawrence-Bailey wedding, there was no need to look at the directions any longer. The decorations lead me directly to the huge tent on a hill overlooking the Potomac. The roadway was lined with dark purple and cream balloons. I noticed a parking lot near the site and found a spot in the back for my ride to rest until the festivities were over. I didn't want to get trapped in the departure traffic.

For early October, it was a really nice evening. We were experiencing a true Indian summer. The temperature was in the low 60s, but the tent was heated to combat any cool air from the lake. Although nice, the weather was still no comparison to the mid 80 degrees in Florida. I'd get home soon enough.

I was ten minutes early despite the traffic. Guests had already been seated. There were a few seats left in the back rows.

"Good evening sir. Are you with the bride or groom?"

I cordially responded, b*ride* and was escorted by a lovely hostess. She sat me near a woman who might have been Erica's second aunt or very distant cousin because she was unhappy about her seating arrangement.

"They put you in the back too, huh?" she remarked with a smirk.

"I don't mind. I was just invited few weeks ago."

"Tacky! See, I told my husband these northerners don't have no hospitality. I used to change Erica's diapers when she stayed with me in Spartanburg and this is the thanks I get. They got some seats up front. See, I coulda been playin' bingo tonight, Cleo. Who child is you?" She turned from the older gentleman beside her to face me with the question.

"Oh, Ma'am, I'm sorry, I'm not family. I'm a friend of the bride's."

She continued to purse her lips while looking me up and down and remarked, "Mmm hmm. See, Cleo, they got us back here with a friend. I'm family. I don't see why——" she continued to rant and rave about her displeasure as if she was Rosa Parks in the fight for civil rights. I just laughed internally and tuned her out. I didn't want to miss Dolly's walk down the aisle on account of a disgruntled family member.

It was a good thing I did divert my attention away from Cousin Sue Ella because the quartet began playing the musical prelude. The processional was soon to come. I looked at the program to read the order of the wedding party. I counted and saw that Dolly would make her entrance in minutes. She was one of two maids of honor.

Cita St. Agathe was the other. I began to sweat knowing that Dolly was soon to grace us with her presence. I obviously wasn't the only one who recognized my nervousness because I found two mysterious pieces of tissue lying on my lap. It must have come from the upset cousin.

When the sun peeked through the clouds, a new sunshine lit my surroundings.

Dolly held white flowers across her arms and a resplendent smile on her face. I adjusted myself in my seat and puffed my chest like a robin on a spring day. Dolly looked great and I was glad I was the one dating her.

After reaching the gazebo, she looked around as if searching for something. She spotted me, winked, and turned her attention back to watch the flower girl drop rose petals as the ring bearer walked beside her. As beautiful as the scene was, I was ready for the reception. I wanted the complete attention of Ms. Darlene Hunter. The wedding guests could have her through the nuptials, but as soon as the head table finished eating I planned to be in her grill complimenting her in her maid of honor splendor.

Vivaldi's Pachelbel Canon played as we stood to receive the bride. I smiled, imagining Dolly's face between Erica's head and shoulders. Then I quivered thinking I was getting ahead of myself. I was a guest to honor Erica. I had to put my selfish ambitions aside so as not to get off track. However, I kept the plastered smile. It seemed the only thing to do when welcoming a bride waltzing to the altar.

"Isn't she gorgeous?" Cousin Sue Ella asked while nudging me.

"Oh yes, definitely," I replied, shaking my ahead affirmatively. All the while, I was anticipating the end so I could get to the beginning of my time with the lovely Darlene. In time, I hoped it would be our chance to dance down an aisle to the tune of a classical song. For the duration of the ceremony, I had to endure the sound of Cousin Sue Ella sniffing. She continuously beat my knee urging me to cosign on how beautiful everything looked. I love family. They talk badly about you and love you all in the same breath. What I loved even more was watching the way Dolly's scarf waved in the wind behind her. I wanted to be the breeze that kissed her neck. Instead, I settled for what I later realized was a kiss on the cheek from Cousin Sue Ella at the end of the ceremony.

"Nice sittin' wit ya, Honey," she said. Her husband didn't seem to mind because he remarked as they were leaving, *Better you than me.*

I was in such a daze I had not realized that the wedding was over. I adjusted myself and rose to my feet as Mr. and Mrs. Bailey walked the aisle once they were pronounced husband and wife. Just behind the happy couple was my flower walking through an autumn evening. Her scent was lovelier than fresh rain on a bed of roses. Her aroma called me and I planned to answer.

CHAPTER FOURTEEN
The Moon Dance

I watched as the moon showed its face.
The river was its mirror.
On this night, it was brighter than the sun.
In one moment I breathed heart-shaped air.

In the fall
I felt cool light.
In the spring
I was left in a trance.
In the summer
I soaked in a splash of comfort.
In the winter
My fears were covered in a blanket of snow.

I watched as the moon waltzed across the sky.
The river was its mirror.
On this night, it was brighter than the sun.
In one moment, I breathed heart-shaped air
And I danced.

*F*or the first time anywhere, I present to you, Mr. and Mrs. Richard Bailey.

Wedding guests cheered and whistled after the deejay announced the arrival of the happy couple. Invited guests were aboard a chartered dinner cruise and cheered and whistled in the direction of the happy couple from each of the three decks. Richard and Erica had their first dance on the pier before boarding the cruiser. As the deejay faded the music, the groomsmen encircled Erica. The familiar sound of a bass guitar began to play. It was the Temptations *My Girl.*

Richard crouched down on bended knee to serenade Erica with a mic in his hand. The groomsmen were his backup singers. The audience roared with excitement. The hosts cued the guests to blow bubbles in their direction. Erica looked like she was in a snow globe with the soapy circles around her. I thought Richard was going to lip sync the song, but he surprisingly had a very nice voice. We didn't know Richard could be so loose. He was more of an introvert than his new life partner. I guess it was his way of showing Erica he could be spontaneous. Her response showed appreciation. Tears of joy flowed from her eyes.

Once the performance was over, the guests met the bride and groom on the main level for the receiving line. Erica's cousin did a great job with crowd control. She had plenty of staff to keep the traffic moving. I guess Erica had a chat with her before the reception. The wedding party stood with Erica and Richard to shake hands while wearing plastered smiles. Mama and Papa Lawrence, Erica's brothers, and a handful of cousins who used to visit in the summer were about as much of the family I knew. Hugging ensued. Giggles from relatives shouting, *You'z maaareed nah*, was repetitive. I thought I would gag if I heard that line from *The Color Purple* one more time. Nevertheless, I held on while waiting to shake the hand of the one who made my adrenaline rush through my veins.

"You look outstanding, Ms. Hunter." The smooth voice of Mr. Washington changed my disposition from crazed maid of honor with burning feet to floating angel with clouds for shoes.

"Thank you, Gerald."

We continued to stare and smile at each other as if we'd soon disappear. The spell was broken when Cita coughed in my ear to let me know there were others waiting in line. He kissed me on the cheek.

"Save a dance for me, pretty lady," he whispered in my ear.

I know I was glowing because there was a bright light shining on the river—or maybe that was the moonlight. At any rate, I was pleased to have received the kiss and the invitation to dance with him later.

Like one thousand fluttering butterflies, I trembled at the thought of Gerald. It was the only thought that helped me to get through the remaining moments following the receiving line. The photographer positioned the wedding party for what seemed a million pictures. I sat through four toasts to the bride and groom. Cita and I flipped for the opportunity to salute our best friend. Cita won the toss. God knew I wasn't in any position to give a speech. I lacked the ability to get mushy in front of strangers.

I was unable to enjoy dinner because I had to display the proper social graces at the head table while rushing through my lightly seasoned prawns, smoked salmon, and broccoli flowerets. The bouquet toss was like a flash in the night, quick and painful. One of the hostesses stepped on my big toe while jumping for the throw away bouquet. I conceded. I liked my feet more than catching the flowers that were supposed to give me hopes of believing I would be the next one to marry.

The cake cutting ceremony was repetitious of any other act during a wedding. Rum cake was smeared all over the bride and groom's faces while they stayed in a kissing position for the photographer. The plum and pearl adorned cake was delicious but I was only able to eat a few bites. My focus: wrapping my arms around Gerald while slow dancing to a classic R&B or jazz tune. Honestly, Led Zeppelin could have been spinning on the ones and twos and I would have still slow dragged with Gerald.

The night was coming to an end. My responsibilities of being maid of honor ceased when the third rotation of *Electric Slide* gave me the clue it was time to sit down.

"Ready to dance?" Gerald asked me.

"Are you kidding? My feet feel like icy hot. They'd probably sizzle if I dipped them in the river." I know Gerald wanted to laugh. Instead, he just displayed a corner smile.

"Tell you what," he began while rubbing his chin.

"What?" I looked up to him with inquisitive eyes.

"Let's go on the top deck and watch the ripples in the water."

"The wind isn't blowing strongly."

He looked around and picked some decorative pebbles out of a potted plant near one of the dining tables. "Then, we'll create our own."

Innovative. I liked the way he used his brain. I was inclined to make waves with him. We climbed the stairway leading to the top of the cruiser. Gerald spotted two empty seats. We occupied them. The air was really cool. He wrapped his suit jacket around me.

"Take off your shoes."

"What?" I couldn't believe my ears. Walking around barefoot in his presence was risky. Exposing my toes was like stripping naked in public. It was a personal matter. I wasn't quite ready to let the dogs out. I tried to be slick and peeked at my pedicure. As I suspected, the polish was already chipping from my clumsiness. The gravel near the pier didn't help my toe job either. They felt like they were in a fight against the earth. My pinky toe was starting to shine like Rudolph the Red Nosed Reindeer.

"I said take your shoes off," he said with loving force without blinking. So, I figured I'd honor his mandate. I responded by unwrapping the laces from around my ankles.

"Okay, you asked for it."

"Girl, nobody's thinkin' 'bout your corns and bunions."

"I don't have corns and bunions, thank you. My feet are just under construction from all this wedding activity."

"Be quiet and hand 'em to me." I did. Gerald sat on the edge of his seat and placed my feet on his lap. He massaged them.

"We'll dance some other time. You've had a long day, young lady. Let me help you relax." Gerald held my feet in his hands and moved his thumbs in a vertical motion while applying pressure.

"Are you flirting with me, Mr. Washington?"

"And if I am?"

"Carry on," I chuckled and commenced to slide backward in my chair and closed my eyes.

Gerald sent me into a state of relaxation. My smokin' feet began to adjust to the movements of his hands and fingers. His massage was like the wheels of roller skates moving back and forth from the ball of my feet to the heel. He moved his warm digits between my toes. He relieved any pain that existed before he took my feet to their resting place, his hands. There was no use in fighting the feeling. So, I let out a sigh. He laughed.

"Feels good?"

"Very."

"How would you like one of these every night?"

"Well, that would require you to occupy space in my home on a full-time basis."

He nodded with a smirk. "Good point. We've been doing pretty well with the self control thing," he winked at me.

"So, tell me, Gerald..."

"Yes, Darlene."

"Tell me the real reason you came to the wedding."

"I was invited."

I hit him on the shoulder for his wise crack.

"No, seriously, why did you come?"

"So I could see you and hold this conversation. I'm addicted to you, baby girl."

"I see."

"So tell me, Dolly..."

"Yes, Sax?"

"Are you always going to be afraid to open your heart, Spider Woman?"

I was taken aback. He had heard that from somebody I knew. There were only three people who used that term, Erica, Cita, and Uncle Jupiter."

"Excuse me?"

"On the real Dolly, I'm digging you. You know this. We're spending more and more time together and my feelings for you are growing."

"Growing?" he interrupted my question.

"Listen, I want to be selfish and have you all to myself."

I was alert. I removed my feet from his grasp and rose from my seat. We both began to look at the river.

"I'm going to make an offer you can't refuse."

I was curious and scared at the same time. Were we reaching a crucial moment in our courtship? Was I looking too much into his words? I felt like I was over reacting. He sparked my interest. Whatever it was he was going to tell me, I felt the need to brace myself for impact. We had been spending a lot of time together. We ate together, prayed together, read scripture together, and frequented just about every lunch spot downtown. The Best Buy attendants knew us because Tuesdays were our DVD days. I found a vintage Atari system and we competed for the high score title for Pac-Man.

We didn't have a title on what we started to develop. He was becoming my best friend but I hadn't committed to anyone in a relationship since JP. I didn't want what Gerald and I had to be complicated because I was afraid that some of my insecurities about relationships might destroy us. I didn't want him out of my life either. I loved the person I was becoming whenever I was around him. I let the wind speak to me, took a deep breath, and slowly blew out spurts of air. "So what's the offer, Mr. Washington?"

CHAPTER FIFTEEN
Vouching for Her

Standing out among the crowd
I'll know my flower anywhere
On land and by sea
Swimming by with other tropical fish
She's my wish
From my "mouth to God's ears"
She will be mine
And On Judgment Day, if allowed, I'd vouch for her
Because she is heaven in my eyes.

I reached in my pocket and grabbed the rocks I found in a flower pot on the main level of the dinner cruise. I skipped them while waiting for Dolly to give in to hearing my proposition. I looked confident on the outside but was nervous and thought she might push me overboard for being so direct. To my surprise, her response came a lot quicker than expected.

"Talk to me, Sax." I turned to face her.

"I want us to be together next Friday at a formal event."

"Where and what time?"

"I have to go out of town next week."

"Okay and...?"

"I'd like you to break your regular Friday evening ritual and meet me for an evening at the Citrus Theatre."

"The Citrus Theatre is in Florida," she declared with an expression of confusion on her face.

"Yes, Ma'am, it is. It's near my hometown in Orlando."

While shaking her head no, she proclaimed, "I don't know, Gerald. Are really asking me to go away with you?"

"With? Oh no, Lady, I said meet me." I then pulled out an airline voucher from the inside of my suit jacket. She reached to view it. "I'm not trying to mess this up." I waved my index finger in the air between us.

"It's an open ticket."

"Of course it is. You can fly out Friday evening as long as you get to Orlando before seven in the evening. A-A-And if you want to go home once the evening is over, you're welcome to leave...no questions asked." She stared at me.

"And if I decide to stay?"

"If you decide to stay, you'll have a room reserved for you and you only at a hotel nearby."

"I don't know," she replied with uncertainty.

"Dolly, at least sleep on it before you say no."

"But Gerald I——"she began with a stutter. I stopped her in mid-sentence by placing my index finger over her lips.

"Shh. Sleep on it, Doll."

"You're something else Gerald Washington. Of all the women in the café that night throwing themselves at you, why did you continue to pursue me?"

"You still have to ask that question after hanging out with me all this time?" I felt myself getting frustrated and began to calm down. I just answered the question while touching her lap. I exhaled. "'Cause I knew you were a dime the first time I saw you in that blue outfit several weeks ago. Three's a charm and it only takes three weeks for anything to become habitual. We've exceeded those 21 days. I'm hooked. I want to make seeing you a habit I can't break. Any interruption in our being in each other's company is simply unacceptable."

Dolly smiled and then tucked the airline voucher under her arm. She placed her palm in mine. I received the right hand of fellowship. Although I'm not a minister, I felt that God was going to make her the First Lady I was seeking.

I faced the river and began to skip rocks again. They danced on the moon's light. Dolly stood beside me. She took a pebble out of my hand and made several poor attempts to skip them too. I felt so bad for her that I demonstrated how we did it in Polk County. I wrapped my arms around her and swayed with the jazz that played below us. Although it was Erica and Richard's special night, I knew the moment couldn't be any more special when Dolly parted her lips and said to me softly, "Okay, I'll meet you."

CHAPTER SIXTEEN
Dressing Up

A good steward is as a good steward does.
I'm taking the next step into this journey of life.
When you run from fate, destiny will find you.
So, I decided to walk into the unfamiliar.
The peculiar.
The Intangible.
Chance?
Of a lifetime?
Or
Misery?
For the moment?
There was only one way to find out.
Stepping out on faith.
I was going to look good doing it, too.

The week leading up to our weekend get-a-way, Gerald and I didn't miss an opportunity to note our every move. My Blackberry was hot. We conversed about anything and nothing at all. He was in convention seminars and I came close to having a few accidents trying to text message him on my way to showing properties. Neither of us was paying attention to what we were supposed to be doing.

On the day of my departure, I was scatterbrained. I was antsy during the closing procedures for my client. Once the last signature was on the settlement papers, I shook hands and quickly made my way through the Pennsylvania Avenue, lunchtime traffic to get to Adore You Hair and Nail Salon.

When Erica and I decided to go off to college, Cita made it her mission to pursue her dreams of establishing herself as a reputable cosmetologist in the Nation's Capital. She studied for her license part-time while we were at Benjamin High. After high school, Cita took a few business courses at the University of the District of Columbia. She learned how to become more innovative in her approach to customer service. By the time Erica and I finished Hampton, Cita's business had generated revenue of over $300,000 in its fourth year with five stylists and two nail technicians. That wasn't bad for a 22 year old. Her investment from the money her father willed to her went a long way.

Her unique Creole décor and services ranging from home cooked meals while you wait and Internet workstations for her clients aided her in the success of the salon. Most of her patronage consisted of college students and high profile professionals. All the amenities catered to women and men on the go. The shop's motto scrolls across the digital marquee, *Make no excuses. Adore You.* It also displays the names of new clients coming in for the day. Cita wants every customer to feel special before stepping into the salon.

"Bonjour!" Cita greeted me as I entered the salon.

"I told you 'bout that foreign talk, Cita."

"Ya know ya like it."

"I wish you'd choose an ethnic group. Creole or southern black?" I held up an upright palm for each of her backgrounds.

"Sit down," Cita said with a kind force.

Since Cita cancelled all appointments after 10 o'clock just for me, I stopped pickin' with her. It was nice to be the best friend of a salon owner.

It was a must for me to get my hair done the day of my departure. I couldn't meet Gerald looking ragged. He hasn't seen me at my worst and I planned to keep it that way. Even on a bad day, I wanted to look tight.

I tried to relax while sitting in the chair. Cita added to my anxiety. She pressed her hands against my head, ran her fingers through my hair, and said, "Gurl, I knew you would need a touch up. This wig is as stubborn as a pair of corduroys in the spring. Your new growth is sticking together like its holding on for dear life."

"Watch it, Tina Marie, not everybody got that good hair like you. My mammy and pappy from the cotton fields of North Cackalacki, baby."

"I'm just saying. Don't wait so long next time, ya here? Now what time is your flight leaving, Doll?"

"Five o'clock."

"Well, I hope you brought a change of clothes with you

'cause we're going to be pushing it since I have to put in some perm."

"I know. I'm prepared. I'll use the shower in the back before we leave," I said while showing her my garment bag.

"No, you'll shower now! You ain't messin' up my masterpiece. Now go on in the back there and grab one of those robes 'til you're ready to get dressed."

Just as I got out the chair, Erica ran into the salon breathing heavily and holding a department store bag.

"Hey ya'll!" We reached out for our group hug.

"What's up, Mrs. Bailey? How was the honey moon?" I asked.

"I'm good, it was good, the sex was great, and I'll fill you in later. I'm just glad I caught you." She started shuffling around with some bags she had obviously acquired from shopping.

"Erica," I began while laughing, "you couldn't wait until the weekend to go shopping? Your husband is going to have a time on his hands with your impulsive purchases."

"Yeah! Yeah! Yeah! But look," she said while waving her hands and unveiling a dress. "I was downtown and saw this in the window of L and T."

The dress was made out of a soft satin with a chiffon overlay. It was accented with red roses on a vine. The split on the side was asymmetrical stopping just below the thigh area. There was one spaghetti strap for the right shoulder. Then I saw the price tag: $450. That was the sale price.

"This is ridiculous, Erica!" I shouted loudly.

"Shh. There are customers in here, Dolly."

"I'm sorry, Cita."

"Don't worry about the price. Richard has enough to cover it. Do you like the dress or not?"

"Gurl, I love it! Where are you going in it?"

"I'm not. You are!"

"What?" I asked with a raised eyebrow.

"It's my going out-of-town present to you. I know your old-fashioned ass...," Erica began but Cita leaned over and interjected in a whisper, "Please, Erica, this is a place of business. I'm going to put both of you out in a minute," Cita remarked while tapping Erica on the butt with a rat-tail comb and then smushing my head with her finger tips.

"Sorry!" Erica shouted in a whisper. "Your old-fashioned tail will probably put on one of those conservative suits and fly out to Florida."

"So!" I fixed my lips in a pouting position because she was right on the money. That's exactly what I had in my bag.

"Don't get me wrong. Your business look is great. I just think you need to let yo titties hang, gurl!" Eavesdroppers in the salon laughed and shouted a series of *I know that's right* while snapping their fingers as Erica shook her bosom. Cita just threw her hands up in retreat and said, "I give up."

"You're not going to meet a client. You're going to be with Blacksax. And this dress screams excitement! I got you some shoes, too, in case you tried to wear those tired ole penny loafers."

"Yeah, Dolly, you need to loosen up." Cita pulled my hair to make her point more clear.

I grabbed the box with the black stilettos and retorted, "Loose? I'm loose. Watch this." I jumped out my seat and started doing the snake.

"Ooh, gurl! Stop!" Cita laughed while waving the comb in my direction. "Just wear the dress, work the shoes, and look beautiful."

"Forget both of you. I got this."

Erica flopped in the leather shop chair and spun around to

face the mirror. I headed to the shower with my bag and heard them still talking.

"I'm excited for her."

"Me too, gurl."

"You think she's gonna give him some?"

"Psst. I'd be surprised. Then again, she was going to wear those loafers, so my guess would be no. She has that thing on lock like Fort Knox."

"You know our gurl!"

"Have for all these years. She ain't changed."

"That's why we love her."

Girlfriends: what would we do without them? Go out looking like a hot, funky mess in my case. Their support made my quest to Florida less stressed. I was going to step out in my new threads in style.

I was blessed to have friends who cared about me. The dress was fierce and I had the attitude to go with it. Cita gave my hair extra body. It was as tight as CiCi Winans during any given performance. Flawless. I was the best dressed real estate agent in town. It was too bad I couldn't share my divaesque look with the rest of D.C.. I had a plane to catch and a man to impress.

Getting through security check at Baltimore Washington International Airport was monstrous. Since the attacks on the Pentagon, the check points before entering the terminal gates continued to get longer and longer. I was glad I had bottled water during the wait. I could have suffered from dehydration before getting to the plane.

My flight to Orlando was waiting at gate B19. I was nervous and excited at the same time. Having that water may not have been a good idea after all. Just as they called for passengers to board, I had to use the restroom. Luckily, a facility was nearby.

Otherwise, I would have to fight with my purse and dress in the hole they call a restroom on the plane. I made it back to the line just in time for them to call zone 2. I was one of the last passengers to board.

I was glad no one occupied the middle seat and I was even more pleased that I had the window view. I didn't want to keep getting bumped from those passengers who roamed the aisle while in flight. There was something about looking out the window of an airplane that calmed my nerves. Although the evening was upon us with the sun closing its eyes on the earth, I craved the opportunity to see the city lights from the sky. I often take for granted the layout of D.C.. Even though the city is full of twists and turns that make driving a challenge, it is still a city with magnificent intentions.

"Welcome aboard Delsouth Airlines Flight 75 headed to Orlando, Florida," The bubbly flight attendant began and then went through the safety rules of flying. Once they start the discourse, I start to pray. I later realized that I fell asleep in the middle of my chat with the Lord. I dreamt that I was hopping from cloud to cloud. I imagined that the gassy masses lead to the steps of heaven. Upon waking from my dream, I hoped the one hour and thirty-seven minute flight would be worth all the anxiety I was feeling. I hoped it would be worth leaving my favorite pair of penny loafers crying in a box made for stilettos. I hoped it would be worth the abuse of sitting near the passenger who was snoring as if three damaged car engines and a sick elephant were revving up his nose. He forced me to go back to sleep.

The next words I heard were "Ma'am? Is this yours?" A flight attendant reached in the seat and held up one of my diamond, teardrop earrings. It must have fallen out while my head was pressed against the window.

"Ooh! Thanks. Can't break up a good pair, can I?" That statement became more symbolic as the evening progressed. It was my personal double-entendre.

All the hurt and pain from the past subsided with the anticipation of having a magical evening in Orlando, Florida. My Fairy God Mother must have waved her wand in my direction because I felt like Cinderella on my way to meet Prince Charming. I exited the airplane with confidence. My strides were intentionally powerful. I suppressed the silk from my web and just started to crawl in a new, open space. The only rapture I wanted to experience was that in the arms of Mr. Gerald *Blacksax* Washington. He was to become my starry knight and I welcomed him into my light.

CHAPTER SEVENTEEN
Soul Food

The bell tolls only when it is struck
By lightening
Radiance Personified
Ascended the stairway to my soul
Doubts?
None for the evening.
Surprises?
Plenty to go around.
Nourishment?
All through the night.
I planned to be full from what she was serving.
A teaspoon of goodness and a cup of Lord have mercy.

My week crept by slowly. Every meeting I attended was inaudible because my mind was clouded with thoughts of Dolly. I shook hands with industry leaders while watching their lips move. Although I didn't hear a thing they had to say, I nodded as if to be listening. I was anxious to see Dolly and hoped she wouldn't go back on her word and stand me up. My final workshop was completed just pass three o'clock. I had enough time to shower, shave, and jump into my tuxedo after getting a fresh cut.

My hometown was Auburndale. However, when I visited Orlando, I frequent my favorite barber. There weren't too many brothers in Polk County who could cut hair. When I got my first set of wheels, I didn't mind pushing the 40 miles for a shape up and tight lines. Clips became so popular the owner had to open up a franchise in the more affluent part of Orlando. The shop's name was later changed to Three In One and serviced both male and female clientele. Leo, the owner, noted in the Orlando Sentinel, *It was only the Father, the Son, and the Holy Spirit that helped me expand my corner barber shop into a thriving establishment.* It was the African American version of Cheers. Three In One was where everybody knew your name.

"What's the deal, Sax? Good to see you back in town." Leo reached out to give me a pound and the official brutha hug. Although approaching fifty, he was still cutting hair like the young cats.

"Nuttin' much. I just finished a week of conferencing." I handed him some recent copies of *Block Writers.*

"Hmm...looks to me by the huge smile on your face the end of the conference isn't the only thang that's on yo mind."

"Well, uh, you're right."

"Sit down and tell me about her."

"I don't have much time to tell you about a woman I've been seeing for a little while but have known for a lifetime in the spirit."

"Ooh, that's deep," another patron said while eavesdropping.

"She must be a dime."

"With change left over, bruh," I replied.

"I tell you what. This cut is on me, Partna! I don't want you to waste any time going in your pockets while trying to get to your lady."

"Thanks, Leo."

I was in and out of the barber shop in a half hour. Leo also threw in a shave to help me cut down on time. I made it back to the hotel by five o'clock. My attire was already spread out on the bed. I jumped in the shower and cleaned up for my baby, Doll. I had a few last minute arrangements to make the evening special. There was no limit to making Dolly feel like the queen in my life. I had to play the role of the king to ensure the palace was fit for a queen. She would, without question, know her position in my life.

Traffic was terrible as usual. It was always rush hour even on the toll roads. Yet, the sweet thought of my sugar rushing into town made the trip easy. I just played back our moments together in my head. It was a welcomed brain freeze. The memories had me in a trance. My smile was bigger than the crescent moon forming in the Florida sky.

I rolled down the window to let the breeze keep me from perspiring. I refused to let her see me sweat. I was Blacksax. I had to remain cool even if I wasn't.

It was 6:45 p.m. when I arrived at the airport. Dolly's

plane was expected to land at 6:55 p.m.. I had ten minutes to position myself for her arrival. I asked her to call me on my cell as soon as she landed. She did.

"Gerald?"

"Welcome to Orlando, baby."

"I have no idea where I'm going. Can you lead me?"

"Gladly."

"I'm walking by Johnny Rivers."

"Great. You should be walking on a mosaic tile in a few seconds."

"I am already."

"Okay, there's a monorail that will take you to the other side of the airport."

"Monorail? Am I near Disney?"

"You're very close to Disney but let's just get you out of the airport first."

"Is it in a little tunnel like thingy?"

"Yes, Ma'am."

"The train is here."

"Okay, hop on it. It'll take you to baggage claim."

"I'm losing signal...I might...you...okay?"

"What? I can't hear you." I figured she was on the train and lost reception on her cell. I had to wait five more minutes before having her in my arms. My handkerchief was working overtime. Man, I was sweating bullets! I had gone out with her several times, fellowshipped with her at a family barbecue, chilled at her crib, and even rubbed her feet. Why was I acting like a school boy on a first date? The wait was killing me. The phone rang again.

"Gerald?"

"I'm here, Dolly."

"I'm almost at baggage claim."

"I'm waiting at the bottom of the escalators, Doll."

I heard in the background, "Enjoy your stay in Orlando, Florida." My heart raced. Suddenly, I had to go to the men's room. I knew things would be perfect. I hoped I wouldn't do anything embarrassing like drool all over her.

"I'm on the platform now."

"Do you see the escalators?"

"Almost there," she replied sounding as nervous as I was.

"Keep coming."

"Uh, Gerald?" She began to laugh.

"What's up?"

"There's a slight problem?"

Oh no! Not a situation. I tried to remain composed and asked calmly, "What's wrong?"

"Don't laugh but I fell asleep on the plane and my contact lenses haven't adjusted to my being awake."

My doll was blind. To ease her concerns I told her not to worry.

"Well, here I come. I'm the woman with the black dress and stilettos."

"I see you, baby."

I smiled and walked toward her. Radiant. I was just a shadow in her spotlight. All I could say to myself was, *It's her.* Her lips parted and her teeth sparkled. I hugged her as if it were our first time meeting. She smelled as sweet as my mama's peach cobbler cooling in a window. I couldn't let go of her. I caressed her hair and looked in her glowing eyes. I could tell she felt the lightning that struck between us. I knew then that my life wouldn't be complete without her. She fed my soul. I kissed her cheek. My lips on her brown skin was the perfect way to start the evening.

CHAPTER EIGHTEEN
Melody Stopper

The darkness fell upon us as we stared at the moon's light.
Not knowing quite what to say, we sat in silence,
grasping hold of each other's hands.
The intensity of the moment paralyzed my thoughts.
The focus ran away with the illumination of the day
My eyes are closed.
My lips slightly open.
My heart is in pursuit of a final destination.

As we stand, the drums of the night are in sync with
the tip tapping of our hearts.
Through the window, we smell the freshness
of our earth
Washing away fears that will take us on this unintentional
journey.
We inhale.
We exhale.
We breathe each other's air.

A vivid memory that has become a movie in my mind
surfaces.
Yet, only you have the tickets to review
This screenplay of reality.

The first hour passes us by and the sun starts to

YOLONDA D. COLEMAN

descend into our world.
As I look back to see your face,
I smile and view your innocence.
And say to you,
"Good evening, heart breaker."

I tried to reach Gerald on his cell upon boarding the monorail train so he could guide me to him. My signal kept fading and we were forced to hang up just as the doors closed. It was so strange to see palm trees and sunny skies when I knew the weather back home was struggling to push 55 degrees. From the window of the monorail, it still looked like summer. It was a welcomed site to see in October.

My cell phone bars were up when I stepped out of the monorail. I called Gerald. He told me to go to a set of escalators which would lead me to him. Minutes separated me from a timeless adventure with Blacksax. I didn't know whether to feel honored or accept the fact that I deserved the courtship that Gerald seemingly planned from the moment we first met.

By the time I reached midpoint on the escalator ride, I lost my concentration because I realized my contact lenses had shifted and blurred my vision. I kept squinting to create moisture in my eyes, to no benefit considering the existing situation. I warned Gerald about my visual impairment. He just told me to relax and said that he was waiting for me at the bottom of the escalator. At that moment my vision cleared. I was comforted and protected. I continued my journey.

It's him. Those were the first words inside my head when I reached the bottom of the escalators and saw Gerald. We swiftly moved toward each other. We embraced. I don't know if my eyes were playing tricks on me, but it seemed that a spotlight was shining in our direction. All eyes were on Gerald and me. Onlookers stared and I felt their smiles. I was in the arms of what I wanted to call home. Could the night get any better?

"I'm glad you made it safely, my little blind mouse."

"Am I really yours?"

"Well, not yet. I'm just preparing."

Everything I needed was in my carry on. It was a very compact traveling bag. So there was no need to waste any more time. in the claim area. I had my bags. Gerald commenced to lead us outside.

Leaning into my ear, Gerald whispered, "You look amazing."

"Thank you, sir. You're not too shabby yourself."

My eyes widened when I saw a stretch limousine pull up to us.

"Is this for us?"

"Only the best. I got this evening covered."

Moisture was building in my eyes. He was doing a good job of convincing me to stay in Orlando for the evening. Rather than making the chauffeur open the door, he signaled for him to remain behind the wheel. Gerald opened the door for me. He held my hand as I tried to get in. I made sure I showed a little more thigh than the dress exposed. Flirting never hurt anyone. He tried to hide his glance but I caught him looking. My lips curled into a seductive smirk to let him know it was okay to look.

The drive to the Citrus Theatre was great. The lights of some of Orlando's attractions were on full blast. Gerald didn't miss an opportunity to explain all the landmarks to me. I had been to Orlando a few times, so I knew a little bit about the city. It was nice to see that the area was still growing.

Although Orlando was hit by three major hurricanes and some of the buildings were still in the process of being repaired, the city continued with business as usual. A quarter of a building's concrete structure was ripped off, partial road signs still dangled incomplete words, holes were in the ground from the from the uprooted trees, and brick walls came tumbling down.

We pulled up to The Citrus. It was located on Church Street which mirrored Bourbon Street in New Orleans. Several luxury cars were parked in front of the theater. At the time, we were the only attendees with a limo. I felt like a star. I stepped out in style. The only thing I was missing was a pair of sunglasses and a personal photographer. Gerald grabbed my hand to help me out of the vehicle. I was careful not to snag my silk pantyhose and stepped down one foot at a time. Just as we closed the door, a young woman greeted Gerald with a big smile, a hug, and kissed him dead on the lips.

"We've been waiting for over an hour."

Gerald replied, "Hey, sweetie. Uh, Melody," he then turned to me. "This is Darlene Hunter from D.C.."

The violins of romance stopped as the strings were pulled swiftly. I tried to remain cordial and extended my hand with grace all the while thinking *I need a quick escape to call Cita and Erica.*

"Hi, Melody. Nice to meet you."

CHAPTER NINETEEN
Grace and Mercy

A monkey wrench was thrown in the plans
Of perfection.
Even at the apex of a terrific time,
The clock stops to let you know
You can never be too prepared.
Grace and Mercy,
Cover me as I fix this mess.

I was trying to wait until we arrived inside the Citrus Theater before introducing Dolly to my sister. Melody was always the perfect scratch on a good record. The tune was playing fine until her excitement ruined the evening. I saw Dolly's face as soon as Mel came up to hug and kiss me. I will admit though, she was still calm even in what could have been a frustrating moment for her. I should have told her that my sister was coming. Mel was just too impatient to wait inside. I could have strangled my sister. She had it honest. The Washingtons need to work on tucking our excitement under our sleeves.

"Gerald and Melody, you guys will have to excuse me. I need to use the powder room," Dolly said with grace but I knew she was pissed.

"Gurl let me show you where it is."

"That's okay. I think I can find it. You two go on and I'll catch up with you in a minute."

I wanted to grab her as she walked away. I shouted after her, "Dolly!" No response. She kept walking in those stilettos that were driving me insane. They hiked her onion up a few notches. Self-control. That's what I needed to keep my mind focused on bigger issues.

"Mel, I thought I told you to wait inside. I was going to bring her in to meet you."

"Big brother, I know. I just wanted to see this woman all the way from D.C. that has your nose wide open. You see Tiffany and Kara taking pictures of the grand entrance," she said in her giddy voice while waving to her girlfriends.

"You couldn't wait five more minutes?"

"No. Besides, Mama and Pops kept pressing me to come out and meet you guys."

"I should have let you stay in the dorms tonight." I shook my head at Melody and then gave her another hug.

She was a sophomore at Bethune-Cookman. I invited Mel and two of her friends to join Dolly and me for the evening. They were still young and ambitious. They drove an hour to party and planned on driving an hour back to Daytona. I was trying to be the cool big brother and let them have fun in style at an industry party. Grant it, a publishing affair won't bring out Nelly and Puffy, but they could still network and possibly get some summer internships.

We walked inside and waited for Dolly to come out of the restroom. She had been in there for fifteen minutes. She was probably telling Cita and Erica what a jerk I was. I had a recovery plan and Melody was going to help me.

"Dolly," I anxiously called her name as she came out. I headed toward her. Mel followed. I got a sharp stare from Doll. "This is my little sister, Melody." She relaxed.

"Miss Dolly, I'm sorry for being so hasty in meeting my big brother. I was just so excited to see him. Being a college student makes you yearn for any family member with cash. He told me so much about you and I——"

I stopped Mel by pinching her on the arm because she was on her way to rambling.

Dolly exhaled, "Oh sweetie, thank you." To my surprise, she stretched out her arms to Melody for a hug. "I'm glad you're family."

Whew! Dolly was back in alignment with me.

"For a minute, I thought you were headed back to the airport for an early departure." Dolly laughed at my comment.

"I was," Dolly's tone was sharp.

"Miss Dolly, please don't go so soon. It was really my fault."

"Okay, Mel, that's enough. Let's just enjoy the rest of the evening."

"Yes. Let's."

I was forgiven. My rose shed her thorns. I had to be more careful if I wanted my garden to be the most beautiful of all. My plan from that moment on was to plan two steps ahead. I wasn't willing to risk any more misunderstandings that evening. I was covered. The enemy was just out to stop that which was good. God's angels, Grace and Mercy, were there to protect all of us.

CHAPTER TWENTY
Soul's Mate

I could spend forever in your eyes
Tantalized by visions of you and me
Making magical memories
Being the envy of passersby
Through your pupils
I learn what fate looks like
What destiny's child will become
Of you and me, us and we, our creation
I could spend forever in your eyes
Looking beyond the surface my
Future is made of chocolate
Covered protection
A spiritual leader
Fighting for his loved ones
I am free to love
So, yes,
I will.
Take my hand and guide me to forever
In your eyes, heart, soul and mind.

SUGAR RUSH: LOVE'S LIBERATION

Talk about a scare. Ironically, meeting Melody stopped my music. It was a breath of fresh air hearing a song of innocence after the smoke cleared. Mel was just excited for her brother. I welcomed the harmony between the two of them. It was a good thing neither Cita nor Erica picked up their phones. I would hate to call back and say, *Gerald isn't a no good so and so...blah blah blah (fill in the appropriate obscenities).*

I immediately thought of Cita and Erica. It's funny how God allows you to see yourself through the reflection of others.

We mingled with publishers and their dates. My smile was a mile wide with each hand shake. I had to support my Gerald. As with any networking function, people continued to reach in the depths of their pockets to pull out business cards. Social etiquette allowed me to take them. *Give me a call,* any given person would say. To release the weight of my purse, I pulled out my card and returned the gesture, *Give me a call if you want to buy property in D.C. or Maryland.* I am never one to pass up an opportunity to sell real estate.

Once inside the Citrus, Melody introduced me to her college friends. After hours of being polite, Gerald and I danced for what seemed to be an eternity. We certainly made up for the dance we missed at Erica's wedding. The band played songs from Elvis to Eve. By the time I realized it, we had burned a hole in the floor. The band had packed up and the only music left was from the radio.

"You're listening to 94.5 FM. We're keeping the romance going as the day comes to an end. So, snuggle up close and relax while we pay some bills.

213

The room went silent. I looked at Gerald and he gave a head nod behind me. I turned to see the janitor holding up his broom while returning the gesture. The familiar tune of an 80s song filled the empty space in the room. Roger. How clever. Gerald held me close to him and repeated the lyrics in my ear.

"Hey lady/Let me tell you why/I can't live my life without you."

Together we sang *Aaaaah baby.* We swayed in each other's arms. I was at home. My fairytale evening was just starting. Gerald was, without a doubt, capturing my heart one note at a time.

"It's 11:45 pm," he whispered softly in my ear.

"I know," I said.

"It was the same time I saw you for the first time."

"I know."

"I can't have my flower walking around without a name tag."

I braced myself.

"Dolly," he began while, holding my chin between his forefinger and thumb, "I want you to be my Special Lady. Whatever hang ups you have from your past, let me prove to you that you'll be worry free with me. I'm making a commitment to date you exclusively to see where the stars will take us."

How could I say no? Hmmph! I didn't. When I confirmed my new walk with Gerald, he kissed me on my forehead. He made his way to my left and right cheeks and then kissed me on my neck. Finally, our lips met. It was our first, official kiss. Two Krispy Kreme doughnuts were melting together and made sugar rush from our heads to our toes.

Needless to say, I didn't take that flight back to D.C.. Gerald kept his promise and checked me into the Georgian

Terrace Hotel. It was down the street from the Citrus, so we walked. The high balconies were atop the stores, clubs, and restaurants on Church Street. Pedestrians could hear the live bands that were positioned in the window.

Midnight had more than made its appearance into the day and people were still waiting to get into some of the parties. It was a live Friday night. Out of the corner of my eye, I saw a man playing the sax by the Orlando Improv. I was walking with my Blacksax and both of us were serenaded into our relationship. I placed a twenty in his hat continued to clutch Gerald's arms.

Once we reached our destination, everything about the Georgian exuded elegance. T. The foyer welcomed us with comfort. The concierge greeted us with a smile. The marbled floors were a perfect contrast to the drapes hugged by gold roping. I looked above and saw the height of the hotel. I felt like a genie in a bottle. Gerald had the driver to drop my bag off before our arrival so, the bellman, unfortunately, was unable to assist us. Gerald tipped him anyway as if he had performed a service. We proceeded to walk to the elevator. We were staying on the 16th floor. The view from the top was amazing. It overlooked the bottom of the hotel. I was released from my bottle and touched the tip of heaven. Gerald grabbed my hand and continued to escort me. We stopped at a door with a red ribbon tied around its handle.

"Your room, Mademoiselle."

Gerald curtsied before me and handed me the electronic key. He kissed me goodnight and headed to his room across the hall.

My room was like an apartment. The full kitchen had a refrigerator stocked with a gallon of cranberry juice. The living room table was covered with back issues of *Block Writers* with a special cover that displayed the silhouette of a woman and a caption that read, *Where's my Dolly?* Draped over the washer in the bathing room was a monogrammed robe. The final surprise was in the bedroom. On the white and gold embroidered Elizabethan comforter lay a single tulip and a note on gold stationary. I flopped on the bed in shear bliss, closed the drapery that hung from the metal cornice and read the note.

To My Lady,

Our foundation started with your note. Now that we've set the bricks on top, I look forward to building more memories with you for as long as God allows. Sleep well. I'll be waiting for you in the morning.

Always,

Your Man,

Sax

My threshold for a new beginning was in his arms and I enjoyed it. He kept playing a love song just for me, so I kept dancing. What was the worst that could happen? Hmm, maybe I would fall in love. Wouldn't that be something?

PART II
THE RUSH

CHAPTER TWENTY-ONE
Break of Dawn

It was a new day
A sweetheart lay asleep
In a chamber created for a princess
Royalties paid in her honor
The price
Innumerable blessings
Prayer
Working in my favor
For the most beautiful girl
In the world
I will gladly submit to
Being whatever she needs me to be
She is my dawn, daylight, twilight,
My moonlight will shine her way
So that she will always be in my spotlight.

Amazing. That's the one word I reserve to refer to the evening Dolly said yes to being my lady. I caught Spider Woman. We were official. I put the stamp of approval on the evening with a kiss.

We both took a late morning flight back to D.C., so we were unable to truly enjoy the moment. I had to attend a charity event at Thomas Jefferson Youth Center and Dolly had a few properties to show. With that said, I didn't have enough time to show her around Central Florida. I did, however, promise Dolly that I would bring her back and give her the grand tour during our next free weekend. Coincidentally, that weekend came faster than we expected.

My sister ran her mouth to the family about how great Dolly was and that we made such a cute couple. Melody hyped us up so much that my parents invited us back to Florida on their dime. Mama made sure to remind us to bring church clothes. No matter what we did Saturday evening, we were going to worship the Lord on Sunday.

During the days leading up to our second sojourn to Florida, Dolly and I came up with new ways to spend our time. We started jogging after work at an indoor track. We had to get rid of the weight put on by our daily lunches. I got a hold of some comp tickets to see a Monday night football game at Fed Ex Field. To my surprise, Dolly was just as bad in the bleachers as I was. Although the Skins got whooped, it was nice to have someone else besides me to throw popcorn on the field when Ramsey threw a bad pass.

DVD Tuesdays continued. There were just some dates that were non-negotiable. We hardly ever finished a movie.

The television would most likely watch us. The guest room was ready to climb into if one of us was too tired to drive home. We bent on the sleepover rule as long as we maintained self-control. Saying *self-control* was our password when things got a little too hot. Dolly wasn't ready to do the sleep in the same bed thing. I respected that. I never pressured her. I just prayed about my thoughts every time I even considered slipping in her room. It was hard (pun intended) but we made the commitment to wait.

My fan base at Blackplatinum started to dwindle once the ladies got word I was seeing Dolly exclusively. It didn't matter because I had all the attention I needed. Dating a regular may not have been good for my image at the club, but it felt good. She was my shining star.

Wherever we went, smiles were shot in our direction. We fit together and there wasn't a person who could deny it. As much as I wanted to piece myself inside Dolly, I knew that was not a part of the Divine order. The fire between us grew with each moment we spent in each other's presence. Kissing Dolly was like tasting chocolate cake right out of the oven chased down with sweet milk. Holding her from behind increased my curiosity. Her neck, my mouthpiece. Her ears, my playground. Her hands, keys to our future. Her stomach, the womb of the earth. Patience tapped my inner thigh of life and I was going to do whatever was necessary to make her happy. If waiting was a part of the process, then I welcomed the challenge.

tsAlthough we were just establishing the second level of our relationship, I was glad she was going to meet my family. I had been around Dolly's friends and some of her family, mainly Jupiter and his wife. It was only fair that those who are closest to me get to know my love interest. If nothing else, it would make her feel like the number one lady in my life aside from Mama and Mel.

Back in the skies two months later, we were both closing out work before touching down in my hometown. We didn't want to play catch up like the last time. During the first half of our 10pm flight, Dolly looked so involved with glasses on, pencil in mouth, and a calculator in hand. I was typing away on my laptop preparing a piece for the Special Valentine's Day edition of *Block Writers*. I was trying my hands at building a series of related short stories—sort of like a continuous soap opera. I wanted to give readers a chance to come back for the next issue to see what would happen next in the character's lives.

"I hope you're not putting our business out there," Dolly said with concern as she sipped her cran-grape juice.

"And if I do?"

"I want my cut, baby." She kissed me and went back to her work.

Every writer puts a little of himself in their pieces. Sometimes, reality is more exciting than fiction. Some things you just can't make up.

Our flight to Central Florida arrived close to midnight. The weather was a bit balmy but still much nicer than it was in D.C. We checked into an all suites hotel near the airport. I didn't want to wake my parents up in the middle of the night. It would be another 45 minutes before we reached Auburndale and those dark roads in Polk County are nothing to play with. We crashed in our rooms until the sun smiled on us once again.

When dawn peaked through the clouds, I got the bright idea to make Dolly breakfast. There was a waffle iron in the suite, so I wanted to put my skills to the test. I jumped in the rental and drove to the 24 hour grocery store. While in the ride, I called my parents to let them know we were back in town. Mama informed me that the family was throwing a cookout. I was quite sure Mama and Pops got on the horn with the family in the Tampa and St. Petersburg areas too. Although an hour and some change away, no distance was too far to travel for the family to get together and break in fresh meat. I'm almost certain the honchos at Male Headquarters would strip my license for bringing a honey to meet the parents so soon. In my defense, however, it was my parent's suggestion. So, by default, I should have been vindicated.

I finished my shopping, quickly returned to the hotel, and got busy in the kitchen. I had Cameo's *Candy* playing on the stereo, put on my chef hat, and prepared a fantastic breakfast. I cooked to the rhythm of the music. I had sense redeemed myself from the Subway sandwiches and Sarah Lee pie Dolly and I had on the Smithsonian grounds during our first date. However, this was going to be the mother of all meals. It was breakfast made with a little TLC.

I had the batter mixed in the bowl. I added some cinnamon to it for an extra kick. Since Dolly was no ordinary woman, I made her the extraordinary omelet with shrimp, onions, green peppers, mushrooms, and bacon pieces smothered in cheddar and mozzarella cheeses. Ironically, the freshly squeezed orange juice was made while jammin' to Kool and the Gang's *She's Fresh*. I wish I could take credit for orchestrating the soundtrack to my movements 'cause they were in sync with each other. I know the neighboring hotel guests were frustrated by the bass of my music but equally pleased with the aroma coming from my room. Whether they were angry or not mattered not to me because Dolly's happiness was all I cared about.

The presentation of the meal was finalized with a garnish

of parsley and strawberries. It was time to make my entrance. Dawn passed and the morning was upon us in full glory. It was 9am. Her smile was the sun to set things right on our path in a new day.

Knock! Knock! Knock! I stood before her door with a tray in one hand and linen napkins draped over my other arm. I had a smile plastered on my face to greet her when she opened the door.

"Who is it?"

"Good morning, Dolly. It's Gerald."

She unlocked the door slowly. I waited patiently and anxiously at the same time. Dolly opened the door wearing an eye patch on top of her head. She put her hair in a ponytail, I gathered, so that it wouldn't get in the way as she slept. She was wearing the monogrammed bath robe I placed in her room the last time we were in town.

"What's all this for?"

"I guess you're not used to being pampered. I am your morning chef."

"Excuse me for a second. I need to run to the bathroom and get myself together. I'm a little caught off guard."

"No prob, baby. I'll just set up out here." The sound of her slippers across the carpet was the sound of innocence. She was scooting. It was cute. I reached in my back pocket and pulled out my mixed cd. India Irie's *Little Things* was the first track to play. It was my subliminal message to let her know the romance won't be dead with me. I wanted to wake up newness in her every time we met.

Dolly came out with her hair down and a pair of blue and grey athletic shorts and a tank top with the Hampton University logo on them. It was the first time I saw her full body and all its dimensions. I always knew she was thick in the waist and that she had a bottom that wouldn't quit, but she was built like an Olympic track star. Her biceps had a slight bulge. Her calves had the strength of a kangaroo. The thighs she complained about were nothing more than baby bearing hips, but they were toned. I didn't cut into her about wearing the oversized jogging suits when we worked out. I just figured that's what made her comfortable. Baby was even hotter than I imagined in my dreams. She could really knock a brutha out if she wanted to. I never would have guessed all that was under her robe. Worldly thoughts tempted me. I wanted to see what else lay beyond the layers of her clothes, but I digressed.

"This is really nice," she said while looking at the spread on the dining room table. The silverware was properly placed on our napkins and our glasses of orange juice were in position. I just needed Dolly to take the seat that I pulled out for her.

"You ordered room service?"

"Naw, sweets. I hooked this up myself. I couldn't give anyone else the credit for this masterpiece."

"Blacksax original, eh?"

"And you know this, woman."

"So, how does it feel?"

"What?"

"Officially being my lady?"

"Well, aren't you anxious? Let's say grace and I'll tell you." We bowed our heads. She extended her hands to mine. She tapped me with her index finger to signal for me to take the lead. I loved that about her.

"So?" I asked while placing my napkin on my lap.

She took a bite out of the omelet. She closed her eyes and chewed slowly. "Mmmm. This is great!"

"The omelet or being my lady?"

She opened her eyes and stared at me with confidence.

"Both," Dolly responded with a beam of light reflecting on her skin from the open window. "I can get spoiled off of this. I hope you can keep it up."

"Well, I'll do what I can."

"I look forward to it."

"I may need to step up my game in the kitchen to keep up with you."

"So you like?"

"I love!"

"Tell you what," I began.

"What?" With seductive eyes, Dolly leaned across the table with her cleavage Ohio 'bout to pop out.

"Uh...girl...come on, I'm trying to be Christian and not reach in and grab you."

"Oh, I'm sorry," she said and then sat back down.

"As I was saying," I adjusted myself under the table. "When we get back home, the next home cooked meal is on me."

"Bet. In the meantime," Dolly wiped her lips with the napkin while speaking, "I want to know what's on the agenda for the weekend. 'Cause I hope we're not gonna just sit at your parent's house and eat barbeque all weekend. We missed out on the tour last time."

"Didn't you know that was the plan?" She smacked her lips. "Naw, for real. I got plans for us." I grabbed her hands and held them in mine. I wasn't sure of her reaction but there was no time like the present time to just drop the bomb on her with no holds bar. "My whole family is coming over to meet you at my parent's house"

"All of your family?" Her voice raised an octave as it squeaked.

"Yeah! Why not? You're here. They're here. I'm just taking advantage of the situation."

"Wow! Are you sure you're ready for me to meet the whole family. I mean, I...I..."

"Baby, if you feel uncomfortable we can cancel and go back to D.C.." I started reaching for my cell.

"No. You know what? I can do this. Let's work this family barbeque thang."

"You sure? 'Cause you know I can just tell my people you don't want their cookin'."

"Stop playing. I'll be fine," she said while shoving a strawberry in my mouth and got up from the table. "Look, I need to get dressed 'cause I want a mini tour of your hood before we hook up with the fam."

"Baby, it's all about you today!"

I finished the remainder of my waffle and took a quick glance at her plate. It was clean. I didn't realize she had finished so quickly. Baby could put it down! She left only the calyx from the strawberries swimming in syrup on her plate. I heard her shower water running. That was my cue to go before I was tempted to take a peek and lose all my inhibitions. She was the sunshine in my city. I liked the sound of that.

CHAPTER TWENTY-TWO
Sunshine City?

Lights beyond the streets
Shine is in the sky above
Tourists fill the highways
Friendships build on bricks
And Sand sifts through the hour
Glass of love.
Strolling through a city of sunshine
With time made for innocence
A cloud presents itself on our shadow
In the Sunshine.

Spider Woman climbed out the web and took residence in Gerald's heart. Surprisingly, it was less stressful than being a spy in the lives of men. Cita and Erica were pleased to hear that I gave Gerald a chance to establish a relationship with me. They were somehow convinced from the beginning that he was what I needed to have a healthy social life with a man. Their carnal minds were telling me to really open up and let him in because I was so uptight.

"He needs to clean out your drain," Erica professed.

I had considered the thought. The last time anyone was anywhere near Lady Sunshine, Bill Clinton was on the brink of leaving office after serving two terms. Ironically, the Sunday morning after my return from Orlando, the sermon was about fornication, the single person's struggle. How convicting. God knew exactly what to put in a minister's spirit just for me.

Anyway, I was more than pleased with my visit to Florida with Gerald. I was surprised when Gerald told me his parents wanted to meet me and went to great lengths to coordinate the flight arrangements for us. Our journey as a couple was just beginning. We were still building and the family wanted in on the action ASAP. I swallowed the big pill and agreed to go. My client's were less than enthused, but I was getting out of the biting cold of D.C. for some more Florida sunshine.

The first morning on our second trip to Florida was a jeans and t-shirt day. The temperature was rising from 65 degrees to a comfortable 80. We went downtown first, but it was dead. So we just decided to take a quick walk around to burn the calories from the omelet, waffle, and fresh fruit breakfast that Gerald prepared for us.

Gerald was really excited about showing me the historical city of Eatonville. At first I had the town mixed up with Rosewood until Gerald broke the facts down to me as we drove through the city.

"This is the first incorporated African-American town in the country. I bet you can't guess which Harlem Renaissance writer was born here." We had just passed the Zora Neale Hurston library. Even if I didn't know the answer, seeing the building was a dead give away. I decided to have a little fun with my sweetie.

"Hmm...you know at the risk of giving an incorrect answer, I am just going to let you tell me."

"Ah...come on Dolly. Okay...look...she was known for wearing hats and it was rumored that she had a crush on Langston Hughes."

"Alright, I'm gonna to take a stab in the dark. Zora Neale Hurston." I had a naïve look on my face. He caught on to my act.

"You knew that already, didn't you?" he playfully sucked his teeth.

"Yeah, I was just pickin' with you. I used to teach English, love."

"I'm sorry, baby," he kissed me on the cheek. "I guess I get a little too excited about literature facts. Don't tell anyone I was trippin'. We straight?"

"Your secret is safe with me."

"I will tell you something you don't know."

"What's that?"

"Before I left Florida I made it my personal mission to raise enough funds to buy a plot of land out here. Look." Gerald pointed to a for sale sign grounded on a cleared plot of land. It was a zoned lot with 3.34 acres of commercial land. Birds were feasting on some unfortunate carcass. He made a left turn and parked on a side street. For a small town, there was still a sizable amount of traffic. We managed to get out the car unharmed.

Half joking and half serious I asked, "Are you planning to operate a farm?

"Sort of. I want to open up a writer's camp for youth." Gerald held my hand and motioned for me to go into the grassy area.

"Gerald, I have on white sneakers. I don't do nature."

"Baby, you'd better get used to it 'cause you're gonna work the land with me until we grow old."

"If anything, I'm going to be working inside as much as possible giving you the thumbs up for a job well done. Did you purchase this land?"

"Not yet. I'm trying to get some investors lined up though."

"I'm impressed, Mr. Washington." If he did close on the property, I didn't know where that would leave me. I didn't ask either. The D.C. area was a little ways away from Eatonville. All I could do was enjoy the journey and let God work out the details.

It was so fascinating to see Gerald in another light. He let down his guard. The Mr. Cool sax player, publisher, business man persona was out the window. He seemed to be at peace in what interestingly enough was his natural element.

"Did you farm as a kid?"

"My family owns a farm."

"The Washingtons are wealthy, eh?"

"We do okay." I could tell by the smirk on his face that he was being modest.

"What had happened was...the land was originally owned

by a white share cropper and slave owner by the name of Sam Charley. The Washington family worked the farm as slaves and as freemen during the start of reconstruction."

"So how did your family come to own the land?"

"Sam Charley died shortly after the Thirteenth Amendment was passed, and he willed the farm to his 16 year old son, Dale Charley. I guess he couldn't handle the fact that his slaves had to be free from the bondage of the plantation."

"Okay."

"Now my great, great, great grandfather, George A. Washington——-"

"So you have the same initials?"

"Yes! Woman, let me finish."

"My bad, baby. Go ahead."

"So anyway, Grandpa George and Mr. Dale used to play together when they were little. As they both grew up, they secretly continued their friendship. In fact, it was Dale Charley who taught Grandpa George how to read, write, and handle money. In front of relatives and friends, Grandpa George and Mr. Dale had to play the role of servant and master. Even though Grandpa George was getting paid to work the field, he still had to be seen as and spoken to like a servant."

"Did this ever affect their relationship?"

"Of course it did. It was the way of the south. In fact, when Mr. Dale took a wife the friendship began to go sour."

"Let me guess, the wife was a true southern woman who wasn't really too keen on change."

"You're on it, Lady."

"I do know a little something about the south." I brought the fingers of my left hand to my lips and blew on them with confidence.

"I hope you'll learn a little bit more after this weekend.

So, anyway, Grandpa George was about 19 years old when he married Dorothy Moss..."

Gerald paused with a look of despair on his face. "Dolly, what's your mother's maiden name?"

"Moss." He grabbed my hand when I realized the possibility of his discovery. The silence between both of us was thick. Paralysis took over. The sun was beaming on us and sweat beaded on both our faces. At that moment, it could have rained and neither of us would have moved.

I tried to assess the situation to decipher why this information had never crossed his mind before. I didn't think to ask for a family history. What were the odds of me falling for a distant relative? It's a good thing we hadn't slept together. The moment would have been even more insane if we had. The sound of a car horn alerted us.

"Hey, man! Move your car out the middle of the road!" Gerald and I rose from the ground, wiped off our jeans, and headed to the rental.

We were riding with no direction. I didn't know where I was but found myself staring into the clouds trying to figure things out. The next thing I knew, we were back on the Interstate.

Coming out of my daze, we had somehow made our way back to the hotel. After turning the car over to valet we walked beside each other like zombies in a horror film. Our eyes had not met since Gerald realized that we might actually be fourth cousins once removed. When I opened the door to my room I immediately got on the phone with my mom. If anyone could investigate our family tree, my mom was the right person for the job. My mother owned *The Moss Family History Book* and was responsible for updating it every 5 years. It was published at the request of my great grandmother during her 95th birthday celebration. When she went on to glory, she willed the responsibility to my grandmother and she passed it down to my mother. I was next in line and this was as good a time as any for me to learn more about the Moss family.

"Mom, can you please look in the index of the family history book for a Dorothy Moss?"

Since I had not told my mother about my escapades with Gerald or even that I traveled to Orlando with him, I was obligated to fill her in on some of the details. I could just see her face. I was sure it was scrunched up in disappointment. She was used to me giving her the scoop on my dates that I decided to keep around. At the same time, I'm sure she squeezed some information out of Uncle James about my potential mates.

It wasn't until I told her about how Gerald wooed me, our date on the Smithsonian grounds, my birthday dinner, the run in with JP, the barbecue at Unc's house, the evening on the dinner cruise, and why I was in Florida on random weekends that she decided to dig into her antique trunk to conduct research on one Dorothy Moss. The facts would still remain a mystery because she had to take another call and promised to get back to me when she was done. Thanks, Mom.

CHAPTER TWENTY-THREE
Relatively Speaking

Is it all relative?
Kissing Cousins Finding
One another on a patch
Of green acres?
Is this some horrible
Dream where the host
Comes out to shout
"You're on Candid Camera!"
Candidly, I am relatively blown
With the possibility of the truth.

What were the odds of Dolly and I being relatives? An otherwise perfect moment was screwed with a tale of my family's inheritance. The silence between us grew like locs, thicker. Our thoughts, impenetrable.

"Mama, lemme speak to Pops." He knew as much about the family tree as the other patriarchs in the family. The stories were passed down from generation to generation. Although I had spent countless Christmas holidays listening to Grandpa Washington's tales about how the family got the farm and how one day it would be mine. I may have missed a minor detail that would solve the mystery of Grandpa George and Grandma Dorothy Moss's existence in our family.

I knew speaking to Pops would be more than a cut and dry conversation. He insisted that he start from the beginning before he would answer any of my questions. That was just his way. I sat back and listened because I knew getting a comment in edge wise was almost an impossibility.

"Son, as the story goes, it was just after the Civil War when Mista Charely passed down the farm to Mista Dale. Grandpa George worked the field as a slave and freeman. Mista Dale and Grandpa George were friends 'cause they used ta play togetha when they were youngins. It wasn't 'til Grandpa George married Grandma Dorothy that the friendship took a turn for the worst. Now, look here, Grandpa George and Grandma Dorothy fell in love the first time they saw each other, but Grandpa George wasn't the only one who noticed her beauty," he continued to go on and on as if to relive the entire experience.

In short, even though Mr. Dale married Miss Sophie, he

still wanted to dip his hands in Grandma Dorothy's cookie jar. One day Grandpa George saw Mr. Dale getting fresh with Grandma Dorothy. Grandma Dorothy could hold her own, and Mr. Dale couldn't stand the rejection any longer. He pushed Grandma Dorothy on the ground as was about to have his way with her. Grandpa George came to the rescue by knocking Mr. Dale to the ground and said, "You ain't no different than your pappi!" Grandpa George grabbed Grandma Dorothy and took whatever belongings they had and left the farm. They made a home in the northern part of Florida with Grandpa George working as a field hand and Grandma Dorothy as a maid.

In 1888, Grandpa George received a telegram that revealed he inherited the farm. An apology from Mr. Dale was also included in that telegram. Mr. Dale and Miss Sophie were never able to have any more kids after their first born died of Tuberculosis. When Mr. Dale learned he was dying, he changed his Will to give Grandpa George the land. 1888 Washington Lane has been in my family ever since.

As much as I love the story, I love brevity even more. I waited until there was a break in Pops' storytelling to get to the root of my concerns.

"Pops, can you tell me anything else about Grandma Dorothy's background?

"Hmm...let me see...," he paused for a minute. "Son, let me call you back and ask yo Aunt Clara."

"Alright Pops, hit me back on the cell."

"Will do, son. Mama wants to speak to you." There was shuffling before Mama got on the line.

"So, wutcha askin' all them questions fo, Doobee?" Doobee was my nickname since I was able to go to the bathroom on my own. Use your imagination for the reason. Sick but that's the story.

"Mama, I'm just tryin' to figure some things out."

"What thangz?"

"Some information."

"Boy, I'll slap you clear through this here phone if ya don't stop playin' wit me. Now tell Mama what's happenin' in her son's life."

"Mama, do you really want to know?"

"I sho do!"

"Okay."

I explained to her how I was giving Dolly a history lesson on the Washington family inheritance when I discovered the name coincidence between Grandma Dorothy's last name and Dolly's mother's maiden name. Although firm and stern, my mother was also quite a comedian.

"Well, if she's your cousin at least you kept it in the family."

"Mama, you know that's nasty, right?"

"Aw, son, you know I'm just playin' witcha. I'm sho everthang is gonna be jess fine."

"I hope so 'cause I really like her, Mama."

"Is she as cute as me?"

"It's like you'd be lookin' in a mirror."

"Oh now hold up...maybe she is family," My mother started laughing hysterically and then I heard a cough from her that was deathly surprising.

"You okay?"

"I'm fine. It's just the weather change."

"Mama, you're in Florida. A 5 degree drop from 80 to 75 could hardly be called a weather change. You'd better get looked at before I come through the phone and get you."

"I know, Doobee. I know. But look, don't worry 'bout Dolly being yo kissin' cousin. I'm sho Snow gone figure thangs out for you." Pops' nickname was Snow because he started graying at an early age. It wasn't until I was almost eight that I found out his real name was Kurt Washington. Even my teachers called him Snow.

"I'm a little nervous."

"Boy, where's yo faith? Just go sho that young lady a nice time 'til the barbecue. The family is comin' by the house 'round three o'clock so you have a while. And by the way, I invited Moses and 'nem over too. They got mad when I told 'em you were in town last time and didn't call. Soon as I told 'em I was makin' my peach cobbla today you were back in their graces."

"Thanks, Mama."

"Now, get off this thang fo ya run up my bill."

"Mama, I called ya'll."

"Oh yeah! Anyway baby, I luv ya!"

"Love you too, Mama."

CHAPTER TWENTY-FOUR
Shared Rib

A spared rib
Was used to create me
Baked to perfection
Browned like honey
Sweet aroma to his nostrils
I will be
Out of the darkness in his Light
The Past burns on life's fire
Sizzling thoughts
Hearts melt
And the ice melts in a glass of lemonade
Everything is cool.

"**B**aby, there's no Dorothy Moss in our family book." The relief that filled my heart was indescribable when my mother parted her lips to confirm I was not related to Gerald. I was happier than a fish that just missed a hook. I jumped up and swiftly ran to Gerald's suite. My knock was frantic. I was just so excited to be able to share the news with him.

"Guess what?" We both said in breathless unison.

"What?" Again with the echo.

"You first," I suggested.

"No you." By this time we both gathered that we had the same news.

"We're not related!" I shouted.

"I just got off the phone with my pops and he said that my Grandma Dorothy's last name was spelled Maws not Moss. There was a little breakdown in pronunciation over the years."

"Now that we're not kissing cousins," I moved closer to him, "how about one?"

"Woman, you don't know how long I've been wanting to hear you say that."

Our lips locked but it was more passionate than our first kiss. I was able to taste Gerald's sweetness and nearly wet my pants. He pulled me closer to him and I didn't back away. The door behind me closed.

It had been so long since I let a man touch me intimately that my body's natural instinct let him take over. His hand crept up my back and I cuffed the back of his head inside my hand. Waterfalls flowed when he tilted my head and swirled his tongue on my neck. My C cup fit perfectly in the palm of his hand. I was melting inside. There was a river in my panties. He pressed his body against mine. I blended in with the wall. He proceeded to unbutton my pants while looking in my eyes and then the same revelation must have come to him as it did to me.

"We'd better stop before we find ourselves in an uncompromising position." He kissed me on my neck. Like R Kelly, *My mind was telling me no, but my body...oooh! My body was telling me yes!* He backed up.

"You're right," I agreed and reached out to hug him. We held each other without movement. I could feel the palpitations of his heart. Mine beat against his chest. I exhaled and we both repeated while shaking our heads in agreement, *self-control.* My eyes told the truth and so did his. Neither of us really wanted to stop. At that moment, knowing that we were not related somehow excited us. Weird, right? I guess it was like a traffic signal. We had been sitting at a red light for a while and once it turned green we pushed the gas to maximum acceleration at the risk of crashing. It felt good until we came to a stop sign and had to look both ways.

Caution was in the wind. My pastor would have been proud that I didn't give in to the flesh or that I had an honorable man in my life who fought temptation for the both of us. It was good to have someone on the team to help make decisions, because I was about to be a loose canon.

We adjusted ourselves and regrouped. Gerald grabbed his bags and motioned for me to go get mine. We requested a late check out. Our time was almost up. We needed to be in a public place. Our hormones were raging. The last place we needed to be was in a hotel with or without separate rooms.

"Are we going back to Eatonville?" I asked as innocently as I possibly could.

"Naw, we're going go kartin'. We have some energy we need to burn off." That was a great suggestion. I wish I had thought of it.

We drove down an entertainment strip known to Orlando residents as I Drive. The *I* was short for International. I Drive was loaded with restaurants, souvenir shops, and an assortment of themed activities for both children and adults. It was like a mini Las Vegas minus the casinos.

Fun Spot was more than a go kart race track. It was more like a carnival for grown folks wanting to get away from the Disney atmosphere. Gerald held my hand and instantly turned into a twelve year old. It was approaching noon and our breakfast had worn off somewhere between Eatonville and the panic of thinking we were related. The sugary smell of cotton candy was starting to take over my taste buds. Somewhere in the air, I was able to sniff warm caramel over freshly picked apples. I was sure giving into my confectionary desires would somehow ruin the barbecue prepared by the Washington family. Gerald gave into his inner child and we both raced to the vending stand that held our cotton candy and our caramel apples hostage.

While waiting for our goodies, I saw familiar faces in my peripheral. They looked like players from Orlando Magic. I nudged Gerald and asked him, under my breath, to confirm what I saw.

"I can't see that far."

"Then we're gonna have to scoot closer."

"And if it is a Magic player, then what?"

"I dunno. Go ask for an autograph or somethin'."

"Baby, let those men and their dates enjoy themselves." I backed down.

We got our candies and moved on to get tickets for the

race track. Gerald paid for three laps around the track and a whirl on the Ferris wheel. We had our choice of four different tracks. Our adventurous nature made us select the biggest of them all. The curves were more dangerous than Beyonce's hips. There were inclines and slopes that forced us to really put the pedal to the metal. My luck wasn't so good when trying to be first to reach the finish line. Out of the three races, I won zero. I did come close to winning when Gerald slowed up to let me catch him. He then decided it was better to taste victory than my dust.

By the time we took our seats on the Ferris wheel, it was 2 o'clock. Gerald let me board our car first. After we were safely buckled in, there was an elderly couple locking lips. I imagined what life with Gerald would be like when our skin wrinkled and we were both sharing Geritol and Fixodent. I wanted what that old couple had.

There was a breeze so I snuggled closer beside Gerald. He adjusted his arm and wrapped it around me. I pressed my head against his chest, closed my eyes, and imagined spending forever in the moment. He kissed me on the forehead and just like the movies, the Ferris wheel stopped at the apex. I positioned my eyes to meet Gerald's and we basked in the irony. On cloud nine, we let the wind blow our car and our hearts rocked to the beat. It was not yet evening but the stars were out. They were in my eyes.

CHAPTER TWENTY-FIVE
Spared Rib

I spared my ribs and chicken
With a side of baked beans
Brown sugar dreams
Sweeten the reality
Once dark like charcoal
Burning on the grill
Hot dogs warm
Cheese melts on the burger
And the ice melts in a glass of lemonade
Everything is cool.

"Dooobeee!" Mama screamed at the top of her lungs with outstretched arms and an apron flapping as she ran towards me. I dropped our bags and gave Mama a big hug. I hadn't been on the farm in nine months, and she held on to me as if it was the last time I'd see her. I noticed that her hair was thinning, which was rather unusual. The women in my family have long, thick hair.

"Hey, pretty girl!" I kissed her on the cheek.

"Doobee, it's so good to see you. Ooh baby, I got some barbecue on your face," she said while wiping my cheeks off with her apron.

"It's good to see you too, Mama."

I escaped the embrace, because I realized Dolly was being left out of all the hugs. "Mama, this is Darlene."

"Ooh, she is pretty. Come give Mama a hug, shuga."

"It's so nice to meet you Mrs. Washington and thank you so much for paying our way here," Dolly greeted Mama and returned the hug. Mama squeezed her half to death.

"Uh! uh! You call me, Mama…everybody else does."

"Okay, then. Mama it is." Mama grabbed Dolly by the hand and led her to the rest of the family and motioned for me to take our things into the house.

While introductions were made, Dolly turned around and smiled at me. It was a silent signal to show that she was okay without me. I wasn't worried. Mama could make a hole in the wall feel comfortable around plaster.

The Isley Brothers were blasting on the sound system as I strolled into the house and saw my cousins, Bug and Noah, sitting in the family room playing bones with my brothers,

David and Nathan. Both my sister-in-laws were in the kitchen watching Mama's peach cobbler and chasing after their children who were plotting to stick their fingers in the cake batter they just mixed.

"That's my point, nigga!"

"Now Bug, you know my mama don't 'cept that kinda talk in this house." I heard my country accent making a comeback. All my education went out the window when I was around the family.

"Yo, man, what's goin' on witcha?" Bug shouted and rose from the chair to give me a pound. He was now rocking small twists in his hair that look like baby locs. "We should jab you in the throat for not callin' the last time you were in town,"

"Yeah, man. We heard you had a honey with you. Where is she anyway?" David interjected while exposing his gold fronts. Nathan came over and slapped me on the back. Noah nodded from his chair, because he was still calculating points to appease Bug, the sorest loser in all of Central Florida.

"You know Mama got hold of her."

"Oh, then, we'd better go on out there and scope her out. She ain't gettin' in the house 'til sundown."

I waved to the ladies in the kitchen. I knew their hands were tied and didn't get in the way of their maternal duties to spank hands and reprimand the cake batter bandits. It was all love. They knew my heart was in my nonverbal greeting.

The fellas went outside to get a glimpse of Dolly while I placed her bags in the guest room and set mine in my old bedroom. Mama and Pops still reserved our rooms for us even after we moved out. We called it the *Big House*. I sat on the edge of my bed and paid homage to the history and memories of the house.

The six room home was built by friends of Grandpa George.

It still had some of its original structure from the late 1800s. Grandpa George was able to later find one of his brothers and sisters and included them on the deed. Thus, the Washington Lane legacy began. Modifications were made to make it more modern so that it wouldn't blow away with hurricane winds. Of course a new plumbing, electrical, and HVAC system had to be installed.

The interior was remodeled by the men in the family. My oldest brother, David, attended a trade school instead of going to a university. He was responsible for putting in the upgrades when needed. They were usually completed for special occasions like Christmas or an anniversary. The contracting company David works for gives him discounts on materials. The owners were friends of the family. The additional labor was usually paid for in glazed ham, fresh collards, yams, and peach cobbler. Mama's food was all the payment David's boys wanted. They figured Mama was doing them a favor.

When my father's generation inherited the land, the brothers and sisters built other homes on it. Pops' two brothers and his sister took an acre of the property so they could all be together. After his kids grew up, Uncle Aeneas and his wife moved to Chicago, and Aunt Clara moved to Cleveland.

Uncle Joe and his wife had untimely deaths. They willed their home to Bug and Noah. They kept the house up but only stayed there when we had big parties. They opted to stay in Tampa where the city life was a little more plentiful. Neither Noah nor Bug got married. They were still enjoying the single life even with 6 kids between them.

During the summer of 1994, the fifth generation Washington Lane owners-to-be pooled our money together to have a lake put on the land. The lake couldn't take up too much space because we still had animals on the farm. The original barn, chicken coop, stable, and a 4 acre pasture for the cows and horses still occupied part of the land. Taking care of the livestock was the only exercise my parents desired. It also gave them something to teach their grandchildren, great nieces, and great nephews when they spent weekends with them. I couldn't wait to have my children work the farm and understand the difference between fresh food and processed food. Farm raised vittles tasted a whole lot different than massed produced food. I exhaled and decided to get a move on. I didn't want to miss the family bonding.

While hanging up my garment bag, I got tackled by two of my high school friends and a former classmate from Stockhem. Ship, Spoon, and Moses all played football for our alma maters. I managed both our high school and college teams. Ship stood six feet two and weighed a whopping 245 pounds. He used to wreck anyone who came in his way on the football field. He was the middle line backer for both our high school and college teams.

Moses was the fastest running back in town. When players saw him coming, they would part like the Red Sea. He was on top of his game until he pulled his hamstring during the fourth quarter to help win the championship game during our senior year. He went to college on an academic scholarship. He was living proof of having a plan B. He finished Stockhem's IT program with honors. Now he owns and operates a computer network firm company in two cities, Tampa and Detroit. The latter was his hometown before attending Stockhem.

Spoon ate anything he could get his hands on but burned it off on the field. For a cornerback, he ate twice as much as Spoon. He ate so much during our sophomore year that Stockhem's head coach put him on a diet. Whoever heard of a football player with food restrictions? We still haven't let him live that down.

"We heard yo ass was in town last month," Ship said and put me in a headlock.

"If you break Mama's bed..."

"I'll buy her another one. Beating yo ass is worth it." Spoon licked his fingers in preparation to hit me across the head.

"The booty better be worth puttin' us on hold nigga!" Moses exclaimed while rubbing his bald head.

"Yo, watch your mouth! You're on sanctified property. And for your info, Darlene is a lady. She's not like those women we messed with at Stockhem." .

"What about Vanya?" The name of my first love in the air made my heart stop for a moment. I had to regroup.

"Now, Spoon, you know better than to mention the V word in front of this man."

"It's cool, Ship." I was turned loose and I fixed my clothes. "Darlene has something that Vanya doesn't."

"What's that? A phat——" I threw a pillow at Spoon before he had a chance to finish the sentence.

"See that's why I can't bring nobody 'round ya'll. 30 and still acting like you're 22. That's why you don't have anybody."

"Wait a minute! I got a woman...well sort of. All I wanted to do was go to the movies and the next thing I know, I'm in love." Moses held his hand to his heart as he looked toward the ceiling.

"Nigga, you ain't in love, you're in lust."

"Spoon, he still ain't hit that. You hit it yet, G?"

"I'm saved, man. I respect Darlene. I'm not degrading what I have with her for some cheap locker room banter." The fellas got quiet. They looked at me. I looked at them. I interjected the silence. "She does have a phat one though!"

YOLONDA D. COLEMAN

We all burst into laughter. Spoon, Moses, and Ship abruptly lowered the volume on their cackling. They then covered their snickers with the back of their hands. I turned around and saw Dolly at the door. I was embarrassed. She had never heard me talking with my boys before. The next thing I knew, Mama entered the room with her palm open. She popped all of us on the head, real hard.

"You boys no better than ta come in here talkin' like that!"

"Dang, Mama! That's was G," Spoon said in his defense.

"I know all ya'll was involved. Now go on out there and help set them tables and chairs on the lawn." Mama left the room chasing Spoon, Moses, and Ship with her one of her sandals.

"Do you need me to help with anything Mama?" Dolly cut her eyes at me while walking behind Mama. She turned around and in a loud whisper said to me, *You need Jesus* I quickly gathered myself and followed behind them.

I knew Dolly would get on me later. For the time being, I was just going to play it off and enjoy the grub prepared by the Washington men and women. It was really nice to see everybody back on the farm.

The kids were skipping rocks, flying Frisbees and riding the horses. Several of the older boys were playing football while the girls jumped rope on the blacktop near the house. Of all the action happening on the farm, Dolly fit right in. She didn't look uncomfortable at all. She was becoming part of the family. I found peace in that.

When the food was ready, Pops rang the bell for everyone to occupy a seat at the picnic tables. The ends of the red and white clothes blew in the wind. The sound of laughter and people rushing to grab the chicken and ribs was familiar.

While the Washington ladies came to the table with the macaroni cheese and freshly popped string beans swimming in a sauna of smoked ham, I was reminded of old times. Only this time, I wasn't a child and a woman other than Mama was fixing my plate. I stopped her and told Dolly she was my guest this time. I prepared her plate for her. She poured both of us a glass of lemonade. Everything was cool. Family, fun, and love were in the air.

CHAPTER TWENTY-SIX
Under Contract

For Sale!
The sign was planted
In the ground.
Passers-by Take a look
Agents send the listing
Walkers on the new carpet
The warranty is proposed
Inspections in progress
Buyers come and go
Vintage interior with a modern exterior
The house stands tall
Through storms
An investor comes and signs
The papers to put the land
Under Contract
Under review while
Another is on the waiting list.

The Washington family was doing more than okay. Colored folks owning property, keeping the family together, and passing the love down from generation to generation was encouraging. I never would have guessed that Gerald *Blacksax* Washington was a farm boy. He really did explore his horizons beyond rural life. Washington Lane looked like a small town with four houses, a barn and plenty of room for the animals to roam. Mama had a garden full of vegetables growing. I'm sure she was able to keep her grocery bill at a minimum.

"Baby, I can't eat them pesticide foods. I grows my own," Mama explained when showing me the fresh collards in the ground.

I really enjoyed meeting Gerald's family. It didn't take long for me to warm up to anyone. The kids had me on the blacktop jumping double-dutch and coerced me into playing tag as soon as Mama finished introducing me.

"Come on, Miss Dolly! You're *It!*"

I tried my best to catch the mini rack stars-in-training. My 29 year old legs were barely fast enough to tag unsuspecting game players.

Gerald's dad, Pops, was busy on the grill and told me he'd *rap* with me later. He was getting his grill on. The Washington women prepared the side dishes and baked desserts in the *Big House*. This was the first barbecue I attended where most of the ingredients were fresh from the potatoes in the potato salad to the butter for the rolls. Aunt Clara bragged about how she spent the previous week preparing and churning it. She flew in from Ohio to visit for a while. She wasn't shy about letting me know it was a good thing Gerald and I came the weekend we did, because she was scheduled to fly back to Ohio the next day.

"Good thing I was here to make the butter. I tell ya, Gloria could do it, but mine is a little creamier. You'll see, Dolly." She adjusted her curly wig and moved about with a slight limp. She later told me how she fell off one of the horses a few years back and misplaced her hip.

"Well, I can't wait to taste your butter, Aunt Clara," I said with assurance. I gathered Aunt Clara was always in need of confirmation. I gained favor in her eyes when I gave the right response.

When it was time to eat, all activities ceased. It wasn't too long before the faces of the children were covered in Mama's famous sauce. Fingers were sticky from the sweet rolls covered in honey. I probably enjoyed my plate more than anyone else sitting at the picnic tables because my Gerald made it for me. I was waited on and I found comfort in that. His gesture made me forget about the macho man comments I overheard in the *Big House* when he was cuttin' up with Spoon, Ship, and Moses. I learned to pick my battles. I was happy to chase my ribs down with a cold glass of lemonade. Everything was cool.

After we finished eating, Pops jumped up and started cleaning the grill. The rest of the Washington family continued talking while the picnic tables turned into spades, checkers, and game board platforms. Gerald's brothers grilled me for a while about my career as a real estate agent. They were apparently trying to get in on the growing market in Polk County. Land was cheap and plentiful since the hurricanes. Plots of land were being sold below cost. It was fun talking shop with them. They were pretty easy on the eyes too. I, at least, knew what Gerald would look like when he was older. His skin wouldn't crack and he'd still have a most of his hair. Even if he started balding, he'd still look good because the gene pool said so.

Pops seemed a little exhausted. He motioned for his sons to help him. The brothers quickly came to their father's aid and finished cleaning up. Pops later spotted me standing among a couple of interrogating women and propped himself from a lawn chair to rescue me.

"Now look here, Ladies, let her breathe."

"Snow, please! We have to break this city girl into southern life."

"Well, Aunt Clara, my family is originally from North Carolina."

"Mm hmm, that's what some of them Ohio folks say. Can't cook a lick of soul food." Aunt Clara slapped hands with Aunt Joelline. Aunt Clara was Pops' sister and Aunt Joelline was Mama's sister.

"Now look here, I'm gonna take Little Darlin' on 'round and show her the animals." Pops felt comfortable calling me *Little Darlin'* and I enjoyed hearing him say it. It was his personal nickname for me.

"I can do that Snow. It's part my land, too."

"Clara, if I ain't know no betta, I'd think Snow was tryin' to get us outta Dolly's face. Come on here. Let's help Sis with the dishes." Aunt Clara and Aunt Joelline cut their eyes at Pops and headed toward the *Big House*. Pops offered his arm and I latched on. We walked behind the other two houses on the property to get to the pasture. Our dialogue was comforting.

"Little Darlin' came all the way from the big city to a big farm. Wutcha know 'bout milkin' cows?"

"Not much, Sir. I just drink the milk."

"What I tell you 'bout callin' me Sir." Pops put his arm around me and hugged me tight.

"I just have to get used to callin' ya Pops." I smiled at him and he returned the gesture.

"Thatta girl!"

We reached the wired fence where the cows were grazing. They didn't smell as bad as I imagined. Although my family was from the south, they didn't have nearly as much land, nor could they afford to take care of any livestock. The most my family had was some collards and tomatoes growing in the ground. Pops told me he was going to *learn* me *how to milk a cow*. He went inside the barn and retrieved a couple of pails. I was about to get a crash course in cow milking.

We washed the udder with warm water and dried it off. He said this keeps unwanted debris from getting in our collection. When he started showing me how to get the milk from the teat he kept saying:

"Now look here, it's 'bout rhythm, Little Darlin'. You gotta feel the beat of the milk from the time ya squeeze the teat to the time it hits the bucket."

I screwed up a couple of times but eventually got the hang of it. Before too long, I was able to squirt two teats at a time. Pops was proud of me. He said the next time I come back, Mama would show me how to make butter better than Aunt Clara.

On our walk back, I asked Pops a few questions. I found it so hard to believe that everyone was so warm to me so early. Gerald and I had just started dating, officially, and I already felt like a Washington. It was as if our relationship was years old.

"Little Darlin', if you caught Gerald's eye, then we like you. That boy ain't brang nare gal 'round here since college."

"Vanya?"

"He told you 'bout V?"

"Yes. He gave me the brief version of the story."

"Hmm, then ya'll need to do some more talkin' but I ain't medlin. Just know that I'm on your side." Pops pulled me closer to him like a caring father.

"I'm sure we'll git 'round to it," I found myself picking up a slight accent. I had to laugh at myself.

"Anyhow, we're a lovin' famlee, Little Darlin'. Everyone we bring 'round has to already be family. Mel loved ya when she first met ya. She told us how ya gave her all kinds of career advice and information 'bout them internships. She has a way of readin' people."

"I just remembered being in college and few people were around to offer me free advice. It was my pleasure."

"Whatever you said had her excited and ready to go on and do that Semester At Sea program. That's why she ain't here now. She's at a seminar."

"Yeah, I was wondering why I hadn't seen her."

"She sends hugs to you. She called not too long ago. She told me to tell you that you could be her next sistah-in-law."

"Is that right?"

"That's right, Little Darlin'."

It was getting dark and the cool winds started making an appearance. As we neared the *Big House*, I noticed Gerald was on the porch talking to someone on his cell phone. I imagined it had something to do with the magazine. I didn't bother him.

The Washington family migrated into the *Big House*. The Al Green, Marvin Gaye, and vintage Motown sound played on the record player for the rest of the evening while Mama continued to yell:

"Ya'll gettin' up in the mornin' fo church. Have ya fun now. Rooster cocks at 5, breakfast at 8."

After the third rotation of *Let's Stay Together*, I took myself to bed.

Gerald and his brothers were playing football by porch light against Spoon and his other school buddies. I gave him a good night salute. He blew me a kiss and whispered, *Thank you*. I didn't quite understand why I was being thanked, but I said you're welcome anyway.

In the guest bed, I curled up with the feather pillows. They smelled of lavender. My slumber was calm and relaxing. No sooner than I was in a deep sleep did that rooster cock at 5am. I couldn't believe it. I tried to sneak a few more winks of sleep, but Mama beat time. She knocked on my door.

"Mornin', Dolly. Get up and take yo bath and iron ya clothes."

Bath is synonymous with a shower or washing up. It's a southern thing. I understood that when I visited my family in North Carolina.

"Yes, Ma'am," I replied with sleepy eyes and a groggy voice. Although my clothes were pressed, I got up anyway. I showered and got ready. I'm sure Mama didn't need any help in the kitchen, but I checked with her anyway.

"Naw baby, I been doin' this for years. You can help clean up them dishes though." She motioned for me to grab the dish rag. It was the least I could do for the hospitality the Washington family showed me.

Mama pulled out fresh eggs and cracked them like nobody's business. Her skills were something to be desired. She poured a cup of coffee with her left hand while cracking the eggs in a bowl with her right. This is all while conversing with me. There were no spills on the counter.

Her kitchen was classic. Pots and pans hanging on the side of the island. The stove was made of cast iron and wood was used to create the fire. She told me Aunt Clara convinced her to get a more modern stove when David, her oldest, was almost six. She did get one but still used the iron stove on occasion. Although a refrigerator stood tall in the kitchen, she still had an ice box. I couldn't believe it. I had always heard stories about the ice man coming around to sell ice for the ice box, but I had never really seen one. *The Big House* was a traditionally modern place. It was a little old school with a little new school.

Gerald came in the kitchen, kissed Mama and gave me a hug. He was suited for church. Pops was still shaving. Mama said he had been moving a lot slower than usual.

"Good morning pretty girl," Gerald began. Mama and I both replied.

"Oh, baby, he was talkin' to me," Mama laughed. I wasn't offended. I had to remember that Mama was the other lady in his life.

"What's up with your hair? Why is it getting thin?"

"Oh, Doobee, you know our family looses hair."

"Maybe the men but not the women. Mama, talk to me?"

"I'm okay. Really, baby. I am getting old now." Mama slapped his hand from taking a piece of bacon.

"But you still look good," Gerald said and kissed Mama on the cheek. "I see the house still don't sleep passed 5 on Sunday mornings."

"Ya know I don't miss Pastor Paul's sermons on Sunday. Oh no! We gotta git our seats."

"Mama you're still sitting in the fourth pew to the right?" Gerald asked while squeezing her cheeks.

"Been sittin' there since 'fore you was born, son."

"Bug and Noah goin' with us?

"Naw, they over at they mama's house. You know they ain't goin' to church. The Lord's still workin' on 'nem."

"What about Aunt Clara?"

"Aunt Clara's flyin' back to Ohio today. She'll be back though, it's snowin' up there."

"What's goin' on in Ohio that she has to leave?"

"Her women's club is having a party tonight. You know how them high society people are." Mama pursed her lips and bat her eyes. She was joking around but we understood where she was coming from.

David, Nathan, and their families made an appearance about a quarter to eight. Both their little girls wore pink ruffled dresses and patent leather shoes. Their tights bunched at the ankle. They hadn't picked up enough weight to hold the nylons. Their little boys had on suspender jump suits and train conductor hats. They knew they looked sharp. Their steps were careful and they smiled from ear to ear. Pops finally made it to the kitchen shortly thereafter.

Mama had the day's schedule down to the minute. As soon as he took his seat, she had finished scrambling the cheese eggs. The sausage gravy was poured over the buttermilk biscuits like snow capped mountains, the bacon and sausage links lay on a silver platter. Pats of butter were swimming in the grits, and the oranges cried citrus tears after being squeezed into the glass pitcher. It was 8am. We blessed the food, fellowshipped, and enjoyed our country breakfast. The dishes were washed. Mama took her *bath,* and then we were on the road in Nathan's Escalade and David's mini van by 10:30am. Service started at 11.

The church was just off a dirt road in Winter Haven, Florida. Most of Polk County, in relation to Orlando, is rural. Television doesn't show you this part of Florida. When I think of the Sunshine State I think of beaches and palm trees, not little house on the prairie.

When we reached the church, I wasn't ready for the massive structure. It was a lot more modern than I anticipated. It looked like one of the mega churches with glass windows back home. It looked like my church. I assumed, from observing the small population of African Americans in Polk County, all the black people probably came to The Second Coming Baptist Church of Winter Haven.

Members dressed in their Sunday best while climbing out of Cadillacs, Buicks, and other fashionable cars driven only for that Sunday drive. These were the cars that stay in a garage until a special occasion arises. Pick any luxury car. It was in the parking lot of the church that day.

Mama ushered us to the fourth pew. There was no need for assistance. I guess everybody knew that was Mama Washington's reserved seat for her family. There were strange stares in my direction. I charged it to the fact that I was a new face. I was cool because that's how my people are. Ya gotta love black folks.

While in route to church, I silently rehearsed my speech for the welcoming of guests. To my surprise, I didn't have to stand and introduce myself. I was only instructed to raise my hand and wait for a welcome packet. I guess the congregation was too big for everyone to stand and give shout outs to their home church.

The mass choir sang classic hymns like *No Ways Tired*, *Wade in the Water*, *How I love Jesus*, and *Amazing Grace*. There were some songs I wasn't familiar with, but I hummed along anyway. Pastor Paul preached from Psalm 23. That has to be one of the most popular scriptures second to John 3:16. I was surprised to find out there wasn't a lot of hollering and screaming. The message was very conversational. Mama said that he's been the pastor for 40 years. He began his ministry at age 18, and he's been at the church ever since. I enjoyed myself. I especially enjoyed watching Gerald thumb through the pages of the Bible to follow along with the supporting scriptures. He shared with me. It was our first time going to church together.

Gerald and I had an early evening flight back to D.C. Mama and Pops gave up the hugs and wished us well on the relationship.

"Ya'll gonna be just fine. I can see thangs, ya know?"

Those were Mama's last words as she handed us a jar of pickled eggs to snack on. As we prepared to enter the airport, the Washingtons pulled off and we waved goodbye.

I could see myself getting real comfortable real fast. I was happy for the first time in years. The inevitable was always a possibility; obstacles were a part of any relationship.

Our flight was scheduled to leave at 6 o'clock. We were dropped off at 4:30pm and my tummy was ready to eat again. However, I wasn't in the mood for pickled eggs. Our departure gate was near Johnny Rivers' Smokehouse. The smell of sweet barbecue reminded me of the grilled food on the farm. I didn't think it would be as good as Pops' ribs, but I was hungry and so was Gerald.

I ordered for both of us while Gerald ran to the restroom. While waiting for the food to be prepared, I pondered on all the work I had to make up for being absent. The weekends were my busiest days, because that was the best time to show my clients properties.

I took out my palm pilot to check my schedule for the coming week. The waiter placed our cokes on the counter. I took a sip, and moments after lifting my lips from the straw, I was grabbed and kissed on my lips.

"Darlene Hunter!" It was my old classmate, Elton *White Bread* Craig, the coolest white boy in a majority black school.

"El, what on earth are you doing here?"

"Vacationing like you, I gather."

"Oh, give me another hug. It's so great to see you." Our embrace was elongated. "What are you doing now?" I asked him.

"Let's not talk about me. You look great, Miss Academia herself. What are you doing these days?" He sat in the chair next to mine. At that moment, Gerald returned from the restroom.

"Gerald," I quickly intervened before any misunderstandings had a chance to surface. "This is El. We went to high school together."

"Oh, what's up man?" Gerald's chest was puffed while shaking his hand. Interestingly enough, for the first time his voice was the deepest I had ever heard it, and that was quite an accomplishment for someone whose voice was already heavy. Was he marking his territory and acting as the alpha male? I imagined so because the next thing I knew, he leaned over, kissed me, and asked, "Baby, did you order the food?" I confirmed that I did.

Elton was proper in that he saw that Gerald was my companion. He gave me his business card and told me to call when I got back in town. We could do lunch. I saw that he too was a realty agent. I never would have imagined. He was a science brain when we were in school. Nevertheless, I was glad to have seen him. He hugged me and told Gerald it was nice meeting him. Gerald gave him a head nod.

Our order came, and we sat silently for the first few bites.

I'm sure Gerald wanted to know if there was anything else between El and me, but didn't dare ask at the risk of looking insecure. So, I helped the situation by talking about how great of a time I had with his family. He entertained my comments, but just as he had some questions about Elton, I too had some questions about his past love, Vanya. In the interim, we enjoyed each other and the last moments of free time before hitting the pavement back home.

CHAPTER TWENTY-SEVEN
Flames

Full Force said it best
"Old Flames Never Die."
You try to extinguish them
So they never rise again.
Somehow they resurface
At a time so inconvenient
And you rush for the end of a pencil
To erase your thoughts
And the poisonous lead reappears
The joy, the pain, the love…
You must make a choice
Act or react,
or be
Proactive.
Even when burned down to the wick,
The flame still sparkles.

It was nice seeing Dolly with the family. Mama and Pops adored her. My brothers told me to be glad they were married, because they would have . Everyone was charmed by her ability to adapt to southern living despite the fact that she was from the north. Pops later told me that he taught her how to milk a cow and she caught on quickly. Spoon and the boys agreed that she did have a nice onion, something Vanya didn't have. Vanya was the last person I brought around my friends and family. Everyone else was just somebody to hang out with. I wasn't thinking long term and therefore kept them out of my intimate circle. Dolly was just as special as V. We were building and I wanted to take our relationship to the fullest extent and prayed things would progress as I planned. Then life happened.

Before boarding, we caught a bite to eat at this barbecue joint. I had to take a leak and headed to the restroom. Dolly ordered our food in my absence. When I was returning, I saw Dolly engaged in a conversation with some white dude. I didn't think anything of it because Dolly attracts all kinds of people. For all I knew, she may have found a new client who might be that million dollar close. The smiles became harder and the hug they shared was that of two people who seemed familiar with one another. *Every night I have to prove my love.* I was reminded of a line in the movie *The Five Heartbeats.* I was cool though. I didn't want to blow up Dolly's spot.

She introduced us. It was some cat from high school. He was looking at Doll with glassy eyes. You'd think she was a slab of ribs from the lunch counter and he was ready to slob her down. I didn't trip. My insecurities could never be made public. Just in case Mr. Craig wasn't aware, I did make my status in Dolly's life known by planting one on her lips and calling her baby. It was a testosterone thing.

Our flight back was pleasant. We were both knocked out. We had been up since the roosters cocking at the crack of black in the morning. The more things changed, the more things stayed the same on Washington Lane. The breakfast was worth it. I wondered if Dolly could make grits like my mama. If she couldn't, we'd be back on the farm in the blink of an eye. A brutha has to have his hot cereal.

Block Writers was up and running when I returned. Regina, an intern from Howard, was able to convince the literary clubs and libraries at American and George Washington Universities to subscribe to the magazine. She was on her way to being a great sales executive. Regina ran a proposal by me to get some of the college students space in the next issue. They were graduating seniors and trying to build their resumes. Although our submission deadline had passed for the next issue, I allowed it. I remember struggling to build my reputation in the publishing industry.

I shot Dolly an email to let her know I was thinking about her before I went through my inbox. I wanted to feed my lady's mind before getting caught up responding to my messages. She usually goes into the realty office to complete administrative work before she hits the ground running. It was her proactive way of providing a quality service for her clients. As she puts it, *I'll look at a property before I even bring my clients to it. I don't show junk.* We agreed to skip lunch that day because we needed to take care of a backlog of priorities missed over the weekend.

My inbox was flooded with messages. I got excited when I saw an email from the mortgage lender for the property in

Eatonville. I only wanted a piece of the 3 plus acres. I had a chance to chat with him while visiting the family. I opened it and he informed me that the price of the land had gone down tremendously. He found some underwriters for the loan and things seemed to be working in my favor. That was the best news for the day. I wanted to tell Dolly but I decided to wait until I closed on the property. My dream of opening a writing camp for urban youth was going to come into fruition.

Somewhere in the midst of subscriber letters, purchase order confirmations, and solicitations from printers was an email from Vanya. I had to sit back and regroup before opening it. Never in a million years would I have expected to see her name in any correspondence marked for my attention. It had been years since I had personally heard from her or seen her. There were Vanya spottings by a few family members and friends. Even when she saw people we knew in common, she never once asked about me. I had no idea what would be displayed on my screen.

Vanya thinking of me? Where was she prior to the night I met Dolly. Talk about a monkey wrench in the plans. I harbored my feelings for Vanya in a vault never to be revisited. However, seeing her name somehow evoked an emotion that made me feel guilty and curious at the same time. I honored the invitation to left click on her name. I tried to prepare for whatever was in the note.

To gerald.washington@blockwriters.com
From sandyv1994@southbellphones.com
Date December 12, 2004
Subject Remember me?

G,

It's been a while. I heard you were in town this weekend. I recently moved back to Central Florida. I just celebrated my 30th. Remember when we first met and we made a pact to marry each other if we were still single at 30? Well, I'm 30 and still single.

We've been through a lot and although it took me a while to forgive you and myself, I'm willing to put the past behind us. Call me the next time you're in town.

777-9311. Just joking. I'm at my parent's house. You know the number.

Love,
Vanya
Your Black Butter

Call her? I wouldn't even know what to say. A small part of me was angry that after all these years she decided to contact me. How strange would it be to see her? What if being in her presence rendered me powerless? I had completely forgotten our innocent pact. In the midst of my thoughts, my cell phone rang. Pops' name appeared on the caller ID display but it was Mama on the other end of the receiver.

"Doobee," she managed to begin through congested nostrils. "Pops is in the hospital. Can you fly back home?" All that was in me was paralyzed.

Everything in my life was happening so quickly. No one could plan an illness and I wasn't about to question God about the recent occurrences of my life. Was this some kind of omen? As soon as Dolly and I prepared to get together there was one obstacle after another.

Mel hastily hugs and kisses me without identifying herself

in front of Dolly. Dolly assumed it's a babe from my past and exits stage left to use the restroom, the most believable alibi when put in an awkward situation. The problem is resolved after finding out Mel is my sister. Things go well for us. I ask her to be my lady and we're supposed to move into happily ever after land progressively. Oh but wait, while enjoying a tour of Central Florida we were faced with the fact that it would be against a moral code to bump uglies because we may actually be cousins. Thanks to the historians in our family, a mere name spelling allows us to continue along the yellow brick road. Things go well. We party hardy on the farm. Once we're ready to take flight back, Dolly gets a coincidental encounter with an old classmate who gave me the impression that Dolly was the blue plate special for the evening; but I'm cool. No problem. She was flying back home with me and showed little signs of interest in anyone else. I get the go ahead to achieve a long time dream of mine. Great news, I can open my youth camp. Bam! An email from a lost love seeps its way through my system bringing back dust filled memories and now Pops is in the hospital. What in the hell did I do in my past life that I became the reincarnate of Job minus the diseases and afflictions. This was the day that Christianity met Buddhism.

I had to clear my head. After working in the office, I went to the Café and played my sax. It was just my luck Jupiter was there too. My emotions were on my face, sleeve, fingers, and any where else they could show up. The last thing I needed to do was discuss my issues with Dolly's Uncle. We established a friendship but family is always going to prevail in any conflict. I tried to keep my composure as much as possible.

"What's happening, young blood?"

"Ain't nuttin' Jupe. How's it bangin?

"I'm just lettin' off some steam. The old lady and I had an argument."

"Oh I'm sorry to hear that, man."

"Yeah, we're fightin' ova who's gonna be on top first," Jupiter started laughing hysterically. He may be older, but his sex drive seems to increase with each day that passes.

"You're a fool, man. I can't mess with you and your episodes."

"Heard you and Dolly had a nice time in Florida."

"Oh, yeah, man. The family did it up right for us."

"That's good to hear. I'm sure Dolly was a hit."

"Yeah, I neva doubted that she wouldn't be. Hey, look here, you gonna be here for a minute?

"Actually, I'm 'bout to go. Takin' Nell out for dinner."

"On a Monday night? Man, football comes on tonight."

"I know. I lost a bet. So, I had to give up the Monday night football game for a dinner with her."

"Yo, that's cold."

"I know. Next time I'm just gonna call the plumba like she suggested stead of trying to fix things myself."

"Good call, man."

Jupiter packed up his sticks and was on his way out.

"Yo Jupe, I'll tape the game for you, brutha."

"Don't even bother. I'll catch the highlights."

I was relieved that I had the Café by myself. Evading any more conversations regarding Dolly and me would prove to be a bit of a task without filling Jupiter in on the current circumstances. I stayed at the Café for another two hours and worked up a sweat. My energy level was up but I didn't feel any better.

Upon my arrival home, I worked out a plan for my second-in-command for the magazine. I didn't know how long I would be out of town but I would always be accessible by Internet. Most of the decisions needing my approval for the upcoming issue were given the thumbs up.

I went online to check for fares back home. The earliest flight I could find was leaving the next evening. I figured it was probably better that I get my CD collection together, a case of bottled water, and see America for 14 hours in my whip. I decided to drive.

Chico was successful at winning the audience over with his skills as the substitute bass guitarist. He also plays sax, so I talked the manager into letting him take my spot until I return. He was nice with his wind too. It was likely I might lose my spot if the ladies enjoyed him. It was cool if that was the case. I had other concerns on my plate.

Dolly had been calling and text messaging me since 5pm and I had not returned her call. I didn't know what to say to her without sounding like an asshole. My mind was a little preoccupied with other thoughts. I really didn't want to talk to anyone but Mama. I spent 3 hours trying to contact the family to no avail. By midnight, Nathan and David had me on three-way. Pops suffered a heart attack and now Mama's anxiety caused her throat to close up. Apparently, her hair loss was tied to her current stress. She knew Pops wasn't doing well and tried to convince him to see a doctor. He wouldn't go.

I shot Dolly an email and told her I'd be gone for a while. I had to rush home. By 3am, I was in my car and on the road. I95 became my hypnotic. I was headed in one direction and would only stop for food, gas, and to drain the main vein. Off I went with my thoughts on mute. The only one who heard me was God. I was in prayer for the longest time of my life. God was trying to show me something. I was traveling in a valley through a storm and it was only the beginning.

CHAPTER TWENTY-EIGHT
Grand Opening Closed

Hurry! Hurry!
Come and enjoy the ride of your life!
Dreams awakened by a shove
An alarm clock ceases the movement.
It was too amazing to be real.
The surreal feeling once covering my being
Was a mirage of what others have
And what I only imagine.
The chase. The catch. The Disappointment.
I'm crawling back into my open space
And closing my arachnid eyes for the evening.
Good night, carnival. It was a nice ride.

W hat in the hell just happened? Gerald and I had a great time in Florida despite the relatively obvious obstacle. Our parting upon reaching home was great. Our routine morning check-in went on as scheduled. Then a break in the norm stormed through my fairytale story. Our usual 5 pm call didn't happen. I later tried to reach him by text and home phone. About my third attempt, I started to worry but went on about my business to get my mind off of him. I figured he may have been busy. Then I logged on to my email account and saw a message from him.

> *To dhunter@dcrealty.com*
> *From gerald.washington@blockwriters.com*
> *Date December 13, 2003*
> *Subject Orlando*
>
> *Doll,*
>
> *I have to go back home. Something came up. I'll be in touch.*

The subject made me smile until I read the contents of the email. I thought he was reminiscing about our excursion. His message was vague and left me imagining all sorts of scenarios as to why he had to leave town and didn't call. I know men have a difficult time expressing themselves but if we were trying to be a team, it only made sense to lean on the other for support. His message was so distant and seemed cold. *I'll be in touch.* No time frame in which he would call was mentioned.

Something came up. What is *something* and why wasn't I privy to know about it? Was it the family? Was Spoon or one of his other buddies in trouble? What was the problem?

I rested for the evening with my eyes constantly in REM sleep. I tossed and turned and kept watching the phone. At 3am, I woke up with a jolt. I called Cita. She supported me and came over.

I got up and made some hot chocolate. I calculated the time it would take Cita to get dressed and drive over. No matter what time of day it was, Cita made sure that she looked great. She would say, *A true diva never lets her public down.* She lived and breathed by her mantra.

My door bell rang and I was surprised to see that her hair was in a ponytail, she was without makeup, and she wore sweats. Apparently she was going through something too. The glam look was missing. Cita wasn't as vocal as Erica and me. She told us her problems in her time. Regardless of what was on her mind, she wanted to help me resolve my problem. She knew I was going to dig into her, but before I could ask a question, she told me to sit down and talk.

I explained how distant Gerald had become so soon after our wonderful weekend together. We didn't have sex so it wasn't a hit and run situation. Being diplomatic, Cita told me that he may be suffering from commitment anxiety. It was a brief period of adjustment for men when things seemed to be perfect.

"Honey, they tend to withdraw and filter to make sure great women like us are real."

"But look at this email." I handed her a printed copy. Cita's Creole side was starting to surface.

"Hmm...Dolly, I don't know. 'Dere's a lot more to

---

this message. Ya shoulda told me about 'dis before my first analysis."

"Okay, Dr. St. Agathe, what's the prognosis?"

"I dunno. Tell me da order of events again."

Sounding like a broken record I explained how we talked earlier in the day and then I didn't hear a word from him again until he sent that dry email. By this time, I had become frustrated because if he had flown home, I should have at least received a phone call by now. If for no other reason, it would be nice to know that he arrived safely.

"Nada damn phone call, telegram, nuthin, Cita."

"Wait 'til da morning, love. He really might be going through a rough time."

"But if we're a couple, I want to support him."

"Men are funny. Let me take dis email. I'm going to meditate on it."

"Are you going to break out your candles and give me a prophecy?"

"Don't discount da power of my Creole heritage. I can see things, damnit!" We both started laughing. It was all I could do to keep from crying.

"You're a trip girl."

"Look, don't lose any more sleep over dis. Go to bed. I'm crashin' here tonight." Cita got up and climbed the stairs to head to the guest room.

"I have your spare key, so I'll lock up when I leave."

"You ain't openin' the shop in the mornin'?"

"JR is comin' in at 7am. Some high powered executive has a board meeting at 9 and couldn't come in last night. So, he's doing her a favor."

'Okay, gurl. I'm gonna check my email again."

"Go to bed Doll!" Cita yelled at me from the top of the stairs.

"Okay. I will."

I turned the computer chair back around and started for my bedroom. It was next to the room where Cita was going to sleep. I knocked on her door.

"Gurl, what? Ain't it enough you got me over here when mother nature is still asleep?"

"I just wanted to say thanks, dag!"

"Oh please. Don't worry about it. Just include it in my tip next time."

"Luv you, gurl!"

"Luv you too!"

The next morning came and went. I busied myself showing commercial properties for a few referred clients. I was tempted to reach out for Gerald again but decided that if I didn't hear from him by the afternoon, I would call on his cell again.

When I worry, I try to keep myself busy. It was a good thing that Erica and Richard invited Cita and me to dinner for the evening. They had something important to tell us. I could barely enjoy my veal for looking at my cell phone every five minutes. I had two missed calls from my mom and Uncle James. I excused myself and went to the bathroom to call Unc. I thought he may have had some clue as to where Gerald might be. He was only able to tell me that he had his boy cover for him in his absence. Unc asked if everything was okay. In an effort to protect Gerald until I got to the bottom of things, I told him we were fine. I'm sure he didn't buy it.

When I returned to the table, Erica broke the bittersweet news to us. She was pregnant. Cita and I screamed and shouted, *We're going to be aunties!* Richard then went on to tell us that he had an offer with a large law firm in New York and they were planning to move just after the new year. My heart dropped. Triple threat was about to become the dynamic duo. Then Cita began to open up.

"Well, since we're sharing news…..," she began but I really wasn't in the mood for any more disorienting news at this time. "I've been feeling really unbalanced lately and got a call from my grandparents in New Orleans."

"Sweetie, is everything okay?" Erica reached out to grab her hand.

"I don't want to put a damper on the party, but she told me I had to come to the Bayou as soon as possible. So, I'm taking a hiatus for a few months."

Did I run an angel over? Had I wronged God in any way? I attended church regularly, paid my tithes, and gave an occasional donation to homeless people at least once a week. My man jetted and my girls are leaving me. What did I do to be left in my valley naked and alone?

I tried to muster the energy to be there for Cita as she was there for me just a little less than 24 hours earlier.

"Is there anything we can do?"

"Just pray for me. I'm not sure what's goin' on but I've been breaking out the candles a little more often. My meditation has increased from three times a day to five times a day." This explained why she was in sweats. Her inner spirit was trying to reach her and there was only one other time Cita was like this, when her father died. With Cita, when something negative happens an abundance of joy follows. Hence, the inheritance she received upon the reading of her father's Last Will and Testament.

"Well, ladies, I don't know what I'm going to do without you." I reached out for a group hug. I was not one to stand in the way of progress. Just as I said that, my cell rang. I rushed to read the caller ID. It was Elton. I was puzzled because I hadn't called to give him my number. I let the voicemail pick it up.

We finished our meal and retired to our respective homes. On my ride to the hacienda, I tried Gerald one more time and there was still no answer. My plan when I got home was to take a long bath. I went to my scorned woman collection and broke out the good ole VHS copy of *Waiting to Exhale*. I found myself waking up with the remote in my mug while the grainy spots appeared on my television. The tape had ended. The cell phone showed no missed calls but the light indicating I had a voicemail was blinking.

The first message was from my mother. She was letting me know they were planning to stay through Christmas. She and my dad were going to spend a few days with Unc, Aunt Nell, and me instead of traveling the world. They planned to leave that Friday morning. The second message was from Elton.

"Darlene, the craziest thing happened. I ran into Jeffrey Robinson. You remember him? Right? Wore a high top fade even after it went out of style? Well, anyway, he said you sold him a house. He gave me your cell. Call me soon. Let's do lunch." No more messages were reported.

Another day passed and there was still no sign of Gerald. I did what any girl in my situation would do. I went on with my life. I got my game face back on and remembered just who the hell I was, Darlene *Dolly* Hunter. Wine me. Dine me. Romance me. Leave me alone. I finally returned El's call and accepted his invitation to grab a bite for lunch. We'd talk shop, reminisce, and I would get my mind off Gerald.

Friday came and I still had not heard from Mr. Blacksax. I had to get myself together. I suited up and got ready to face the world as my old self. I looked in the mirror near my door and smiled. I was back. How could I let myself go for something so uncertain? I wasn't that lucky to really meet someone who was totally into me. Men liked the thrill of the chase. He caught me. Game over.

I took an extended lunch with Elton. We had some catching up to do. El made reservations at the Mayflower Hotel. He picked me up from my office on New York Avenue and suggested that I leave all work related items on my desk. Reluctant to do so, I downloaded some files to my PDA. I always had to be prepared.

The air seemed new to me. It's like the curse of the wicked one had lifted. I was in mourning for a few days over the M.I.A. move brought on by Gerald What's His Face. Downtown D.C. was live with men and women in suits rushing to acquire their midday meal. I stood in the front door of DC Realty, Inc. with my Burberry coat and a pair of Versace gloves. My beret covered my head and was cocked to the side as if I were a world renowned model getting ready to grace the streets of Paris in my thigh high Nine West boots. I was fly. The sun was out, so the sunglasses were on. Neither an FBI nor CIA agent had anything on me. This sistah was clean.

El pulled up in a black 700 series BMW similar to Gerald's. His license plate read *REAL T*. Rather than ushering me to the car, he double parked and opened the door for me. He always did have class. I assumed the position as a passenger and waited for him to close the door once I was safely nestled in the beige leather seats. I was comfortable.

"I'm glad you could make it Darlene," El said while taking his skull cap off and rustling his hair with his hand. It was coal black and layered. I liked the change. His hair was long like Cher's in high school. He wore it in a ponytail. It was his personal protest against his parents who wanted him to cut it so desperately.

"I'm glad you asked."

"So, how is…what's his name? The guy who was in Orlando with you? You still together?"

"Oh, we're…" Just at that moment, my cell went off. It was Gerald's number. I placed the phone on vibrate. I wasn't feelin' him at that moment. I was busy. He could wait since I had to wait. Petty but necessary.

"Darlene? You were saying?"

"Uh…," I started stuttering because I had to collect my thoughts. "He's fine, I guess."

"I see." El dismissed my response and carried on. "Well, you look fiiiine today. You always had a sense of style," he tapped my leg with the back of his glove. "Did you know I had a crush on you at Benjamin?" It was no holds bar with El. I had never known him to be so aggressive.

"No. I wasn't aware of that. What I was aware of was the fact that every Monday you wanted me to help you with your English and math homework."

"That was my way of getting private time with you. My work was already done by the time I got to school."

"So you mean to tell me that time you brought me roses for helping you pass Tyson's test had an underlying meaning?"

"Fo sho!"

"And the time you called my house junior year begging for me to help proof your term paper was an act?"

"What can I say? I was in the drama club."

"I should beat your ass for that. I missed *Livin' Single* for you that night."

"My sister still has old episodes on tape if you're still interested in watching them." I was flattered. I never would have imagined having this conversation with El almost 12 years out of high school.

"So how did you get into real estate, Mr. Physics?"

"It was something I just fell into shortly after college."

"Where'd you go again?"

"Dartmouth. Anyway, I invested in a rental property while living at home with my parents. I moved into it after paying off most of the principal and became interested in helping others become property owners."

"So, you didn't go into the science field at all?"

"Oh yeah! I was a research assistant at the ACS."

"The ACS?" I was unsure of the acronym.

"The American Cancer Society. It was a personal decision to work there. My mother fell ill to breast cancer while I was in school and I wanted to be involved in seeking a cure."

"I'm sorry to hear that. Did she survive?"

"She sure did. We sought some alternative treatments and they worked. The chemo was killing her faster than the cancer. In her honor, I participate in the Komen Race for the Cure each year."

"That's nice of you."

"I still do. Wanna go with me next June?"

"Let me think about it, okay?"

"No pressure." El looked at me with a glowing smile. He grew into his looks 'cause he had an Orlando Bloom appeal to him that I was digging.

"Your mom is lucky to have a son like you."

"Well, she's the special woman in my life, right now." He looked at me out of the corner of his eye as if to send a subliminal message. I maintained my posture. I couldn't send off any mixed signals. Timing was everything.

"So, you're not seeing anyone?" I asked.

"Nope."

"Any kids?"

"Only the ones I volunteer with on Saturdays."

"You volunteer? Where?"

"I help out with an SAT program at a charter school on Minnesota Avenue."

"You're kidding me? Knight Senior High?"

"Yeah!"

"I used to teach there when I came back after college."

"Where'd you go to school again?"

"Hampton University. As beautiful as Hampton is, I decided to come back home." I bowed my head while fluttering my eyes as if to seem shy.

"Hmm. How about that? Look how fate has brought us together." El grinned and held my hand at the same time.

My phone vibrated again. Gerald's name was on display. He was now becoming a distraction to my lunch. Too much time had passed and I wasted too much energy trying to get in touch with him. He'd have to wait. I turned my phone off.

My lunch with Elton was like a hot stone massage, relaxing. My troubles seemed to go away as we remembered prom and the National Honor Society meetings when everyone jumped at the chance to volunteer on Thursday because that meant an early dismissal.

We reminisced about the time we took the same Hi Skip class at George Washington University. Hi Skip allowed advanced students in high school to take selected college courses for credit. Instead of taking an academic course, we took an art theory. El and I enjoyed the luxury of having access to the collegiate activities even though we were still in high school.

"Remember when we used our college IDs to get into the Ritz?" El reminisced.

"Yeah, and everyone was looking at us like we were crazy?" I cosigned.

"What is she doin' with that white boy? Ah man, that was a trip!" he laughed hysterically.

"What was even funnier was your poor attempt to do the running man on the dance floor."

"Yeah, it was pretty awful," El admitted.

"Maybe it wouldn't have been so bad if the dance wasn't dated."

"Hey, give the people what they want, right?"

"A good laugh?"

"Exactly!" El snapped his fingers, pointed in my direction, and winked.

After our lunch, El and I promised to stay in touch. It was nice to clear my head with fond memories from the past. My smile returned, so I celebrated by treating myself to a brand new pair of shoes. The mall and I became friends again and my soul was beginning to rest. It was 6pm. My parents were in town and life was good. I shouldn't have let my groove get disturbed so easily. The risk you take in love is that there is always the possibility of getting disappointed. God's son was shining in my direction again and that was always guaranteed love.

CHAPTER TWENTY-NINE
911

911
Emergency
Family in crisis
Not knowing the vices
That lead us to His graces
911
Emergency
Strokes at Midnight
Mother hears her son's cry
and I never knew why
I didn't respond to the call
911
Emergency
Love's past comes to haunt me
My feelings fall deeply
For the one whose heart is empty
911
Emergency
A jump start is needed
The warning was not headed
I fell asleep
And now I am bleeding
My heart calls out to her.

I arrived at Auburndale Memorial Hospital at 5pm on a Tuesday. My brothers, Bug, and Noah were sitting in the lobby sleeping. Mel walked in behind me. She was coming from school. Pops was on IV and Mama was on a breathing treatment. We weren't allowed to go in at the time, because they were still running tests on both of them. I wish I had arrived sooner.

"David?" I pushed my brother awake.

"Yo, G, when'd you git here?"

"I just pulled up."

"Did you fly?"

"Naw man, I had some air to clear out. I drove."

"Here, man," my brother rose from his seat. "sit down a minute."

It was another forty-five minutes before a physician or nurse came out to give us an update. We were allowed to go in two at a time. The family let me go in since I had just come in town. Nathan came with me.

They placed both Mama and Pops in the same room. It only made sense. Mama had tubes extending from her mouth. She was asleep when I walked in. Pops was barely coherent but was able to speak to me.

"Hey, G," he managed to say in a whisper.

"Pops, don't talk. Just put your thumb up or down. Feeling any better?" He put his thumb down. "You gonna be strong enough to get outta here soon?" Thumbs up. "Want a beer?" Thumbs up. It was nice to know he hadn't lost his sense of humor knowing good and well Mama made him stop drinking a long time ago.

The doctor came in and said that if their tests came back negative, they'd be able to leave in a couple of days. For the moment, they were both under watch. Nathan said Pops was feeding the chickens when Mama noticed he had fallen on the ground. If he had exerted any more energy during the barbecue, we may have lost him. The doctor said that bed rest was mandatory for a few weeks, and Mama had to take medication to help her with the anxiety attacks.

We stayed at the hospital for another three hours and then we headed back to the farm. David and Nathan went to their homes. Bug and Noah came back with Mel and me to the *Big House*. Mel assumed the position of Mama and cooked dinner. She didn't feel like staying on campus. It was interesting to see my little sister in a domestic capacity. I always knew she had grown up, but looking at her maneuver her way around the kitchen made me proud. She was no longer a little girl. She was becoming a responsible woman.

I offered my assistance in the kitchen. It was the least I could do. The house had run out of things to drink. She asked me to run to the store to pick up some sugar, lemon, and tea bags. Bug wanted to ride with me. I was too hard headed and told him I could make it. I was just going down the street.

I had to remember my way around the Winn Dixie. It had been so long since I shopped in Auburndale. Surprisingly, some of the same cashiers still worked there. One of my high school classmates had assumed a management position. Cheryl Laven was a star cheerleader turned Winn Dixie associate. She and her squad would always pick on me. Since I wasn't playing ball like Spoon and Ship, they joked that I would be their manager flunky friend for life. *Success will always be the sweetest revenge.* I learned that from a friend of mine.

Cheryl recognized me but seemed embarrassed to speak.

I waved to her and it forced her to wave back with a half-cornered smile. I already had enough going on in my life rather than be worried about high school insults.

On the return trip home, I remembered to call Dolly. I then remembered that I left the cell at the house. Moments later, I started seeing a mirage of trees form around the highway. One thing Florida needed was some street lights on the county roads. I knew I was tired, but I didn't know I was too tired to make a trip to the store and back. The mirage kept closing in on me and I became hypnotized. The next thing I remember was the sound of Mel screaming. I had flipped my car over in a ditch.

72 hours before my parents would be released from the hospital, I was admitted. Life was still and the only thing I could think of while the doctors tried to fully revive me was that I needed to contact Dolly. The light around me went black, and a SOS signal was sent to anyone who could hear it.

I finally woke up that Friday morning. Standing before me was a woman in red. She was holding my hand.

"Sweetie, I heard you were in the hospital." I couldn't make out the face, but I recognized the voice. It was a familiar angel.

"What day is it? How long have I been here?"

"It's Friday. I came from Tampa this morning." I remember smiling and calling out Dolly's name. The hand holding mine was released. At that moment, I realized it was Vanya. I knew then my time with her had expired. Pact or no pact I made a commitment to be with Dolly. She was all I needed. I closed my eyes and remained silent in my thoughts about Darlene Hunter. She would be my focus after getting out the hospital. I hoped my spirit reached her and she would respond and be by my side soon.

CHAPTER THIRTY
And A Heart Rings Out

Prophecies
Tell stories of what's to come
Patiently
I waited for an answer.
Angels
Were used to deliver God's message.
Faith
Is needed when life seems hopeless.
Promises
Kept when you trust Him.
Repent
And be restored.
Of all the Lord has to offer,
The greatest of these is love.

U nc and Aunty cooked a ham, greens, and potato salad for my parent's arrival. We dined together and played Uno until the wee hours of the night. We were chilling out. Dad said they realized that with all that's going on in the world, they'd better stay put on American soil and be close to the ones they loved the most. Instead of flying around the world or circling the globe by way of a cruise ship, the plan was to have Christmas dinner at my house. I was going to cook and give Unc and Aunty a break and mess up my kitchen for once. They would stay with Unc and Aunty for part of their stay and they would stay with me for the remainder of their time in the D.C. and Maryland areas.

I was climbing into bed around 4am when my cell rang. It was Cita.

"Dolly, call Gerald."

"What?"

"Dere's something wrong. It has nothing to do with your relationship. I was meditatin' today and in my mind's eye I saw IV bags and blood."

"Cita, you're tripping me out."

"Gal, if ya luv ya man, call him not now but right now. Ya here?"

My mom walked into the bedroom as I was on the edge of the bed on my knees and my face turned to heaven.

"Baby, what's the matter?"

All that was in me finally surfaced into tears. It was then I realized that Gerald's departure had affected me. I was so busy trying to seem like I didn't care that I had not yielded to my emotions. Mom had the true spider sense. She knew exactly what was wrong without me saying a word.

"Sweetheart, as concrete as we make love, it's really abstract. No matter how educated you are, you'll never understand its mystery. Follow your heart and have faith." My mother kissed me on the cheek and left to join my dad in the guest room.

I checked my voicemail for the first time since that Wednesday. I had two voicemails from Gerald's number and one number from an 863 area code. Melody was calling from his number. My heart sank when I heard the message. My Gerald had been in a car accident and was in ICU. The last message was left 24 hours ago.

I spoke to God that evening before going to bed and prayed it wasn't too late for me to get to Gerald. I was taking the first thing smoking to Central Florida. It didn't matter the cost.

Uncle James and my mother dropped me off at BWI. I was frantic. They told me things would work out. While waiting to board the 6 am flight, I called the *Big House*. David answered the phone. I told him I would be in Florida at 8:30. He assured me that somebody would be there to pick me up.

For the first time ever, I didn't fall asleep on the plane. I just prayed and prayed until the wheels of the plane screeched on the runway. I packed light. I had my purse, a tooth brush, a pair of underwear, and some deodorant. I would worry about clothes once I found out Gerald was okay.

Bug and Noah picked me up. They briefed me on everything that went on. They told me about Gerald's parents being hospitalized and how Gerald drove to Auburndale as soon as he heard the news. My baby was working on zero sleep to rush to his family's aid. This explained why I hadn't heard from him.

Gerald had some broken bones. The doctor's were able to stop the bleeding. I was warned that he suffered a lot of scaring to his face. Bandages covered his face to help heal the wounds. His car was totaled but he was saved. Praise God.

When we got to the hospital my heart raced. I was paralyzed while walking the hall. A woman in red walked by me and smiled. People were so friendly in the south. I returned the smile. Room 333 was where I found my love. He lay there helpless. I felt horrible for thinking Gerald was trying to ditch me. I walked closer to him. He was a mummy, but he was my mummy. The only parts not covered on his face were his eyes, nose, and lips. I kissed him after bypassing the IV tubes that were attached to his arms.

"Gerald, baby, I'm here."

He opened his eyes. I was hoping he could see me clearly.

"Dolly, I love you."

"I love you too, Gerald."

CHAPTER THIRTY-ONE
Completely Incomplete

Surgery was performed.
Dr. JC renewed my valves.
Before stitching me up,
He said it was time to restore my spared rib.
I slept.
In the morning, I was made whole.
I was to be complete.

She kneeled beside my bed and prayed for me. She refused to leave until the nurse forced her to go home and get some rest. In my weakened state, she gave me the spiritual energy to endure the pain so that I could once again hold her in my arms.

The holidays came and went. Christmas was spent in Auburndale. By New Years, I recovered well enough to head north and bring in 2005 with Dolly's parents. Surprisingly, I wasn't nervous about meeting them. Knowing I was already in good with Jupiter made it easier for me. He told me to just be comfortable and not to put on a façade. *Be yourself,* he said. That wasn't a problem.

Dolly mirrored her mother's looks. Mrs. Hunter's sandy brown hair mixed with gray lay passed her shoulders. It was a beautiful contrast to her skin that gave off a sunburned glow—Dolly's mom was a looker. I see why Mr. Hunter ran her off to the mountains of New York. He wanted his honey all to himself.

Mrs. Hunter was shorter than my Dolly and often had to tiptoe to reach the cabinets in Dolly's house. Mr. Hunter, however, stood taller than the refrigerator. Dolly fell somewhere in between the both of them. I jokingly named the three of them small, medium, and large. Mr. Hunter kept his hair close, like me. We had something in common. I felt at home.

"Now, Darlene, that boy got a good head on his shoulders, cash, credit, car, no children, and his own crib? I'm 'bout to buy you a ring for him." Mr. Hunter shouted to Darlene in the kitchen. He then slapped down an ace of spade to cut Jupiter's king. I was Mr. Hunter's worthy partner.

"What are your intentions with my daughter, son?"

"Nothing but honorable intentions, sir."

"Now, what are your honorable intentions?"

"Whatever God has in store for me, I want to share it with her. She's the most precious diamond I could have ever selected," I said as I placed down the red ace in that suit. I winked at Mr. Hunter and he understood.

"Well, alright. We're gonna have to talk more about these intentions after the game. Do you fish?"

"Yes, sir. I do."

"I like this boy, James."

"I told you he was a good one, brother-in-law," Jupiter cosigned to Mr. Hunter's comment. We won 300 to 180. We set Jupiter and his partner back a few hands and rose from our seats in victory.

I finally told Dolly about the land in Eatonville. She was in my corner every step of the way and spread the news like wild fire to whomever she could. After closing on the land, I had to make several trips back and forth to Florida to get the center constructed. I hired a public relations firm to help me with fundraising. Think Inc. was without a doubt the new buzz among Central Florida's youth.

Applicants anticipated its grand opening for the summer. I was also able to coordinate a partnership with the Orange County School System to allow students to earn community service credit during the academic year. They would able to write, design, and publish a quarterly newspaper for residents in the community.

Everything was going according to plan. The center was opening with its first session in July. TSC Public Relations coordinated a party at the World Plaza. Second Chance Bank, one of the largest black owned financial institutions in the southeast region of the United States, donated a sizable amount to Think Inc. They also sponsored the opening reception. This was a great marketing move for us because other notable businesses came to our aid. They truly believed that *children are the future.*

I also had a future to be concerned about and tried to secure it just as soon as I reached the roof of the World Plaza with my lady. Although I felt complete with all things great happening, I was still missing one thing. I had to put that piece into my puzzle of life.

CHAPTER THIRTY-TWO
Love's Liberation

Sparks fly in the night
From a knight
Without a horse
But on foot
And I fall into his arms
And thank the heavens
For restored faith and trust.
The chains are broken.
My heart pumps blood again.

I couldn't have been more proud of Gerald. He was seeing life's ambitions through. While he was working on Think Inc., I finally closed on that million dollar deal. During Christmas in Central Florida, I befriended a developer who was interested in property in Potomac. I helped his wife comfort their toddler when the oversized Mickey Mouse character moved in for a hug. He was most appreciative. We built a relationship and when he came to visit D.C., we met for lunch.

"Dolly, I like your style. You're passionate about what you do."

"Thank you, Mr. Padgett."

"I'll be ready to move my things in my new home by July. Make it happen for me." He dropped a signed, blank check on the table. We shook hands and concluded our meal with a toast. By May, a contract was signed and we closed on the 2.5 million dollar home a month later.

TSC Public Relations sent me an elaborate invitation for Think Inc.'s opening reception. Cita and Erica joined me at the request of Gerald. They obliged. Erica, in her third trimester, took a flight against doctor's orders.

"Girl this baby will okay. She's got strong roots!"

Cita's journey to New Orleans was becoming a emotionally draining. She declared that a mini vacation would free up some mind space. Gerald reserved a suite at the World Plaza and we made it Girl Trip '05.

Knock! Knock! Knock! "Baby, it's me." It was Gerald. I rushed to the door to see my honey. As soon as the hinges folded for entry, he planted one right on my lips.

"Dolly, I missed you." He squeezed me until our hearts beat as one.

"It's only been two weeks since we've been a part."

"Two weeks too long! Where ya girls?"

"Hey, Sax!" Erica waved as she waddled around the corner with grapes in one hand and a bottled water in the other.

"Heeeey, Erica!"

"Richard said congrats and sorry he couldn't make it." Gerald slid over to rub Erica's tummy as if she was Buddha!

"She looks like she's 'bout to drop, don't she?" Cita questioned while reaching in to give Gerald a hug.

"Ladies, thanks for coming through. This means a lot."

"Please, you're practically family, Brother Sax." Erica winked at him.

"Look, I just came up to check on you guys. I have few things to tie up before the evening. So, I'll see you at 7 sharp. Cool?"

"You got it, baby." I hugged Gerald and he kissed me on the forehead.

Erica, Cita, and I hit the outlet mall. I told them about all the bargains I got the last time I was in town. Baby Erica was going to be the most stylish infant in New York. Richard's credit card was burning up. Cita racked up on shoes. I was disciplined and just bought an outfit for the evening. A new dress for my baby's new dream.

7pm. Food, fun, and music. All the students who were accepted for the first summer camp session at Think Inc. joined us. They were honored with laptops provided by Moses' IT company.

"I just love tax right offs." I was in earshot when Moses whispered to his companion as they walked toward the elevator.

I continued to mingle with the crowd. In the midst of a conversation with the president of TSC, Gerald excused us and gestured for me to follow him. With a smile, I submitted to the request. He grabbed two glasses and headed for the elevator.

"Where are we going?"

"There are some people I want you to meet upstairs."

"Upstairs? This is a big party, baby."

"It's an important time for us. I want you to be a part of it all."

The elevator stopped on the top level of the hotel. We then took the stairs to the rooftop. As Gerald opened the door, both our family and friends sat amidst balloons and white linen table clothes weighted down with champagne flutes. I looked at Gerald in amazement. He ushered me to keep walking to a pedestal.

"Thank you all for coming out to celebrate this evening with me as I open Think Inc., the first African-American operated writing camp in Florida," Gerald spoke into a microphone. He then proceeded to take a bucket of water from under a table along with a brick.

"As complete as this Fourth of July celebration might appear, my work isn't done and my life can't be complete without having this lady beside me." He crouched on bended knee.

"Dolly, I wash my hands of all those who came before you." Gerald dipped his hands in the bucket of water. Moses gave him a towel to wipe his hands dry. "There is only one brick left to insert into the building of my life. Will you please do me the honor of helping me lay the foundation as my wife?"

Tears streamed down my face as I screamed, *Yes!* Just at that moment, the fireworks from Disney exploded into the air. We kissed. Gerald held me. Flash photography became our sunlight. Whistling and clapping were in surround sound. He was the one. There were no reservations about it. One of the last thoughts my brother shared with me was *Don't be with the one you can live with, be with the one you can't live without.* Gerald was that person.

It was a Friday going into a Saturday when my world began to flip inside out. It was 11:45pm when Midnight stood before me. It was the evening of Independence Day when Lady Sunshine merged with the Moon. Together we would be powerful. Together we would shine.

Then, in the midst of a glowing moment, winds came from the south. The woman I saw at the hospital appeared in the doorway.

"Vanya?" Gerald whispered in surprise.

Damn, my heart cried. Even in liberation, there is still a struggle. It was time I took a stand for love. What God has brought together, let no man or woman separate. Let the spinning of my new web begin.

ROLLING CREDITS

THE INSPIRATION

It gives me great pleasure to share my baby with the world. Sugar Rush: Love's Liberation was conceived on my cousin's 26th birthday, June 9, 2001. I remember several attempts to conceive this project beginning in 1999. Dolly and Gerald were works in progress until the day I found their voices. I hope you enjoyed their story as much as I enjoyed creating it.

Gerald Washington's dialogue was inspired by men who helped me think like a man as much as I could being a woman. Dolly, hmm, people will ask if I'm talking about myself. My PR response is, *Every writer puts a little bit of himself in their pieces.* Is Sugar Rush: Love's Liberation totally fiction? Let's just say its fictional reality. *Wink.*

The proposal was inspired by a special couple in North Carolina. The Walters made me believe in love. When I first heard about their engagement, I sent an email to Mrs. Walters and told her that I wanted to use it in my writing. I appreciate them for allowing me to share their love with my readers.

THE STRUGGLE

Sugar Rush was not easily released. The project had to undergo years of Lamaze coaching, several false labors, endless labor pains, and a near death experience (a virus on my laptop had the manuscript inaccessible for weeks); but like Ms. Celie in the *Color Purple*, it may have taken forever, it may have caused me to sacrifice some time, but it's here! There were times my baby was in ICU fighting for life. Just when the enemy wanted me to pull the plug, God stepped in and said *Who's the Master?* I replied, *Sho Nuff!*

SPIRITUAL DISCLAIMER

I wrote this love story with a ministry in mind. I am totally responsible for Dolly and Gerald's spiritual walk. However, they are tempted and make decisions accordingly. They remain my role models as I try to be more like Him.

Their friends? Well, they are who they are and they tell it like it is. It's easy to be holy and sanctified when you don't face temptation. Everyone around you isn't saved but you try to walk on the straight and narrow as much as you can. You can't give the praise if you've never gone through trials. God used me to tell the story for those who know the struggles of being single. If you are such a person, this one is for you!

ACKNOWLEDGEMENTS

God placed people in my life to make this journey easier: My family and extended families, my editors in the 20774, my roots in the 20020, S. D. Haskins, R. Padgett, Gamma Iota, NHAA, Inc., FECA students and faculty, Elite Hair Designs, Sweet Tooth Bakery, Three In One staff, The Peoples Film Company, Zoe Force, The Bell, Barry, and Jemison-Barnes Experience, Baadchuck, Polarity Networks, Dwale, Family Pressures, The Georgian Terrace Hotel, JRA Media, and everyone from New Milford to Tampa. Please forgive me if I didn't mention you by name. Please charge it to my head and not my heart.